D1282727

A STRONGER CLIMATE

By the same author

AMRITA

THE NATURE OF PASSION

ESMOND IN INDIA

THE HOUSEHOLDER

GET READY FOR BATTLE

LIKE BIRDS, LIKE FISHES

A BACKWARD PLACE

A STRONGER CLIMATE

9 STORIES

R. PRAWER JHABVALA

W·W·NORTON & COMPANY·INC ·

NEW YORK

Library of Congress Catalog Card No. 68-13486

Acknowledgements are due to *The New Yorker* in which IN LOVE WITH A BEAUTIFUL GIRL, PASSION, AN INDIAN CITIZEN and THE MAN WITH A DOG first appeared; to *The London Magazine* for THE YOUNG COUPLE; to *The Cornhill Magazine* for A SPIRITUAL CALL and A YOUNG MAN OF GOOD FAMILY.

PRINTED IN THE UNITED STATES OF AMERICA

1 2 3 4 5 6 7 8 9 0

FOR *Catherine* AND *John*

"They come no longer to conquer
but to be conquered."

Contents

I

THE SEEKERS

In Love with a Beautiful Girl

Although after a few months there the idea of India was still exciting to Richard, the place itself and especially his daily life in it had become dull. He had rented an expensive, up-to-date flat in an area full of other such flats and of people (mostly non-Indians) very much like himself in status, income, and way of living. Even when he went visiting away from this area, it was only to go to similar places with similar flats and similar parties and similar people giving them. Life for Western man, it seemed, ran very much to pattern in India, and so did Western man himself.

Richard, however, was not used to thinking of himself as identical with other people, and he certainly did not find much point of contact with his colleagues at the High Commission or with those others who made up the circles in which he was expected to move. They all seemed to him very much in the tradition of the white man in the colonies, and the fact that the tradition had been modified did not make any fundamental difference to their personalities. Nowadays they were expected to pay tribute to Indian culture as exemplified in art, architecture, dance, and so on; to have some (carefully selected) Indian friends; occasionally to serve Indian curries at their parties: but these requirements once fulfilled, they were free to follow their natural inclinations and speak disparagingly of the weather, the servants, and – after the Indian friends had gone home – of the Indian character.

The only apparent alternative to this, Richard discovered, was to go eccentric. One eschewed the social round and concentrated, Indian-style, on developing the soul, or the self, or whatever it was that clamoured for deliverance. This was the way taken mostly by unattached lady secretaries at the High Commission or librarians of the British Council, who took to wearing a sari and travelling round the country in third-class railway carriages. Most of them went very eccentric indeed and were not a pleasure to know, but there were exceptions, and one such was Mary with whom Richard became friendly. She was not the sort of girl he would have chosen if the range had been wider. Himself slender, lively, and good looking, he had a leaning towards very decorative girls, and decorative Mary decidedly was not. She was heavily built, with big hips and legs, and the clothes she wore did not minimize this defect. She had nice eyes, though – clear and of an honest blue – and an easy manner that won her many Indian friends. She was good-humoured about letting eager Indian youths get into conversation with her in public places, and she would invite them home to her flat, and they brought their friends, and she played the gramophone and mixed drinks for them and let them read T. S. Eliot aloud to her.

She and Richard had a pleasant friendship together. They had the same sort of (liberal) mind and agreed on basic attitudes, which made them automatically allies in the colonial-style English society in which they found themselves and in which these attitudes were by no means common. They spent much of their free time together, and they always found something amusing to talk about, even if it was only the antics of their fellow-Britons. They also liked to talk about India and swap their impressions of the country. It was an agreeable friendship, though in many ways dissatisfying to Richard, especially when he stopped to think how many hours he spent having amusing conversation with Mary in her or in his own smart flat, with the up-to-date décor and the air-conditioner going, when outside lay what he had grown up to think of as the most passionate, beautiful, and mysterious country in the world.

When therefore he met Ruchira, he was more than ready for her. She was beautiful, to him mysterious, and, he was sure – it could not be otherwise – passionate. He courted her assiduously and was well received. Fortunately, she came from a family that prided itself on being modern and forward-looking, so that no difficulties were put in the way of his meeting her. On the contrary, he was encouraged to visit the house frequently, and whenever he did, he was first held in conversation by Ruchira's father, who had been at Oxford and liked to talk about those halcyon days. The house was large and beautifully kept by many unobtrusive servants – full of flowers and chandeliers and, here and there, tiny glittering golden gods kept apparently for decoration rather than devotion. The family was an exceptionally good-looking one, with several handsome brothers running up and down the stairs with tennis rackets or driving away at top speed in sports cars. The mother was elegant and faded, with an air of melancholy because she was an ageing beauty and an air of distinction because she came from a royal house and was called Princess. These graceful people and the graceful house in which they lived were, for Richard, a most pleasing setting for the jewel which was the object of his attentions. Here Ruchira's charms were seen to their full advantage – what better place for her laughter to echo in than these tall airy rooms, her willowy young figure to move in than that garden of velvet green lawns and old trees? It was all an ideal he might have dreamed of in his undergraduate days, or before that, when he was a schoolboy and wrote poetry, but even then could hardly have expected ever to find.

Ruchira, however, thought her home dull and old-fashioned and longed for those worlds of Western sophistication to which she hoped Richard would introduce her. He did, in fact, introduce her quite soon to Mary, and this was a great success with Ruchira. She loved Mary's flat and all those books, she sat on the floor and had a gimlet and a cigarette and said how much at home she felt. Actually, though, she did not look very much at home: she was too glamorous for the place. In silver ear-rings and a very soft silk sari of white and silver, her long wide eyes brilliant with excitement, she sparkled like a crystal chandelier fit for some raja's palace but not for Mary's modern intellectual apartment. The gimlet took quick effect and she talked rather more and more freely than she might have done without it. She spoke of her love for literature and her longing for – she couldn't quite express what, but for a life different from what she had hitherto experienced, a life of books, thought, emotion, and, above all, of interesting people. She wanted to meet many interesting people, artists and writers and such, famous tennis players, film directors, anyone indeed who had ever done anything memorable. She asked eager questions about Paris, which had always been her ideal (the painters, the pavement cafés) and to which her father had promised to send her as soon as the foreign exchange situation eased a little. She would study something there, she wasn't yet quite sure what. Of course, painting would be the most logical choice but art had never been her best subject. What else was there? Literature? Leather-work? Perhaps Richard and Mary could suggest something? She looked up at them eagerly, radiant, and Richard was grateful to Mary for being charmed by her and answering her quite seriously, weighing possibilities with her.

Afterwards, when Richard drove her home, they were

both of them intoxicated – he with her, and she with three gimlets and the exciting evening she had spent. She said she liked and admired Mary very, very much, she asked a lot of questions about her, she said she had always wanted to meet someone like that – intellectual, well-read, there were not many such people in the world Ruchira's family inhabited. Her brothers and their friends, she said, didn't care for the intellectual life at all, only sports and dancing and a good time, that was all they wanted. And her mother – well, he knew what Mummy was like, never opened a book in her life and when she saw Ruchira reading would tell her she was spoiling her eyes. So to meet someone like Mary was a revelation, and such a nice person too, and she wasn't really bad looking, her eyes were good and perhaps if she dressed a bit better – but of course a person like Mary could never be bothered to think about clothes, that was too silly and frivolous. Ruchira too had no time to spare for people who thought of nothing but what to wear. Richard, driving his car, glanced sideways at her and said, 'That's a marvellous sari you've got on,' and she looked down at it, smoothed it over her lap with an involuntary little smile. He stopped the car and regarded her with the frankest admiration. 'Are we home?' she said, peering out of the window.

'Nearly,' he said. He got out of the car and went round to the other side and opened the door for her. 'Would you care for a walk?'

She was first astonished, then delighted. '*Cra*-zy!' she exclaimed as she got out of the car. They were outside a park that was locked, but it was easy to climb over the barrier. He leaped over first, then turned to help her get across more carefully, so as not to rip her sari. Her hand lay lightly in his, but she hardly noticed; she was busy looking down at herself to make sure nothing happened to her sari. When she had got safely over, she exclaimed '*Cra*-zy!' again and, with a laugh, ran ahead of him down the path in a spirit of adventure.

The deserted park had a sixteenth-century mausoleum in it, and was flooded with moonlight. Ruchira, a slim shape glittering in white and silver, ran swiftly over the grass and up the steps of the mausoleum, but she didn't go in. It was dark inside, though the stone tombs could just be made out as three long, eerie shapes by the moonlight that filtered in through the latticed walls. She stood in the entrance and gave a little shudder. He said, 'Awful to be dead, isn't it!' Bats squeaked high up in the vaulted dome.

'There is an Urdu couplet,' she said. 'It goes, *Jin ke mahalon men hazaron rang ke* something, something . . . Very beautiful. I'm so fond of poetry but I have a terrible memory. These are very old tombs,' she said. 'Hundreds of years. How old is Mary?'

'Hundreds of years.'

'Stupid.' She gave him a chaste little push. 'Doesn't she want to get married? Will she always stay single, you think?' And before he had time to say anything – 'Does she believe in free love?' She looked at him eagerly.

He wasn't very old – about twenty-five – but it was many years since anybody had seriously asked him anything like this. He looked back at her in loving amusement and countered her question with 'Do you?'

He saw her expression change: a moment's doubt, fright, mixed with excitement, flitted across it. Then she laughed and ran away from him down the steps of the mausoleum. He followed and sat down on the lowest step. 'Well, do you?' he said.

She stood in front of him and, looking up at her, he saw her head flung back, her throat in a curve of defiance. 'I hate our system of arranged marriage,' she said. 'I don't want that. I want to be free like Mary, and I want to love also and to be loved.'

'Sit down,' he said, and she recklessly did. Now they were so close together that he could feel her warm body breathing. She was very excited, but brave too; she looked straight into his face and dared him to do his worst.

He kissed her. Her body was tense and her lips dry, but she kept quite still. She had a superb smell, which was not only perfume but something else too, more mysterious and feminine than anything he had before encountered. Her soft, dusky skin also felt different. Perhaps it was because she was Indian, perhaps because she was more beautiful than anyone else he had ever kissed. He took his lips from hers and buried his face in her hair.

But she had had enough. She pushed him away – which was easy, he was so weak with love – and got up. 'Mummy'll wonder what's happened. She always waits up for me – I've told her hundreds of times don't, but she's so – be careful, there is a ditch here, that would be funny if you fell in, wouldn't it?' All the way home she was in a much better mood than he was. In fact, she seemed distinctly pleased with herself, excited too, and full of wonder and admiration at what she had allowed him to do.

Richard liked to think of himself as a cool sort of person, and he was. True, he had always been fond of girls and had a flair for affairs – he was rarely without one – but he had always known how to measure himself out, how much to give and how much to keep back, so that these liaisons, although never short on emotion, did not consume a larger slice of his life than he meant them to. With Ruchira, for the first time, he lost control. His response to her was more abundant than anything he had known before, and flowed, moreover, beyond the girl herself into the country that was hers and which became now in his imagination inextricably part of her, so that he no longer knew where it was Ruchira he loved and where India. Suddenly, after months of lying quiet, his feelings for the place took fire. He listened to Indian music, not evaluating it coolly as he had done before, but with a leap of the heart, feeling Ruchira herself or his rich feelings for her in each strange, throbbing note. He visited museums and looked at frescoes and sculptures, and although Ruchira herself was slim, willowy even, he identified her with those heavy-breasted, wide-hipped Hindu beauties and revelled in their sensuousness because he thought it was hers. But it wasn't only in art and museums that he sought and found her: it was everywhere – in the streets, the sky, the air, in flowers and water and trees. Sometimes, mad with longing, he would get up in the middle of the night and go out into the streets to savour the silence there, and the sky and moon overhead, and a ruined mosque with a jasmine bush growing in its compound. He read many Indian legends and became acquainted with many gods and tried to understand about the silver and the shell, the serpent and the rope. The smell of incense filled him with desires.

Mary, however, talked about Ruchira just as if she were any other girl. She even compared her with all those youths who came and read poetry in her flat and listened to records – 'Not,' said Mary, 'because they're all that keen on literature and music but because these things stand in for a glamorous cosmopolitan life'. Like Ruchira, she said, what they really enjoyed were the gimlets and the cigarettes and the doing something different from what everybody else they knew did. Richard argued that that wasn't unlike adolescents anywhere, to which Mary agreed but said that what made it strange was the certainty of what they would go back to when this phase was over for them. 'Religion, caste, joint family – the lot. They'll be as staunch supporters as everybody else.' And Ruchira? he asked. He loved talking about her and hearing her talked about, no matter what was said. 'Oh that's easy,' said Mary. 'She'll marry someone rich and buy a lot of beautiful saris.' Richard laughed; he could not claim that this was unfair and left out of account Ruchira's spiritual riches. He didn't believe in those spiritual riches, didn't in fact want them for her: she was enough as she was. And he liked the idea of her buying a lot of beautiful saris – he could see her doing it, in some expensive shop, surrounded by silks and obsequious salesmen, with a deep look of satisfaction in her eyes.

He always enjoyed visiting her in her house. The whole atmosphere of the house pleased him – that sense of leisure, money, and unquestioned status which had disappeared in England before Richard was born but which Ruchira's family still enjoyed as an unshakable birth-right. Ruchira's father poured Scotch whisky for Richard and talked to him of the Oxford he had known in the thirties, of his wine merchant there and his tailor and his dear old bedmaker, Mr. Norris. And Ruchira's mother, the Princess, who was to be found at any hour of the day in her drawing-room drinking cups of tea from a dainty tray and wearing long diamond ear-rings, would invite him to join her. Conversation with her was strange but not disagreeable. She would ask his views on compulsory birth-control or some such topic of current interest, and in between there would be long silences while she stirred her tea and sighed and looked out of the window. What Richard liked best was to sit with Ruchira on one of the verandas overlooking the garden, on a swinging sofa that was large and broad enough to sleep on and heaped with cushions. They would sip iced lime-water and look at the huge leather-bound family albums, at the photographs of Ruchira's paternal grandfather in a high stiff collar and a pince-nez, or her maternal one smothered in gold brocade and a turban that came down almost over his eyes, cross-legged under a canopy and having a fly-whisk waved over him.

But Ruchira quickly grew tired of sitting at home doing nothing and demanded to be taken out. At first she was satisfied for the two of them to go on solitary strolls in romantic ruins, she picked flowers and wound them in her hair and urged him to recite English poetry to her. But after about half a dozen such strolls – during which, incidentally, she allowed each time one kiss, none of them ever leading to anything further and each one of exactly the same quality and duration as the first – she asked for something more exciting. What she wanted most was to be introduced to interesting people, and she was always questioning him not only about Mary but about all his colleagues and their wives and anyone else he might know from other embassies. But he did not want to introduce her to any of these. They were too dull, pompous, conventional, not worthy of her, and he steadfastly refused to let her accompany him to any of the dreary cocktail parties and receptions that he had to attend. The only party that he ever took her to was an 'unconventional', non-diplomatic one given by Mary: and this did not turn out to be enjoyable for Ruchira.

What had she expected? Certainly, it appeared, something very different from what she found. The party was to have been very informal – gay, if possible – and with this end in view cushions were strewn on the floor and the latest hit records played on the record-player. Nevertheless the atmosphere remained formal, strained even, and the guests seemed unable to relax. They were mostly the young men who so often came to visit Mary – students, clerks, airmen – and who normally made themselves very much at home in the place. But today they felt constrained because it was a party, and they knew that for a party one had to behave in a certain manner of which they were not sure but hoped to pick up the clue as they went along. Also, none of them seemed to have realized how informal the affair was meant to to be and had come in what were rather obviously their best suits; these made it difficult for them to relax on the floor, as they usually did, and though they tried their best to look easy against the casual cushions strewn all over, the creases in their trousers kept them stiff as cardboard. All of Mary's social tact and easy manners failed to get the party going. Every now and again her determined efforts induced a little spurt of animation, but it always died down very quickly and left the guests eyeing each other suspiciously or staring into space with a constipated expression. Even those who were usually very friendly together were today like people who didn't trust each other, and, above all, like people who didn't want to be caught out: wary tourists trapped on unfamiliar territory.

Ruchira did not sit on the floor but stiffly on a chair. Like the other guests, she was dressed too elaborately for the occasion, in a pale rose brocade sari and rather a lot of priceless jewellery. Her eyes were lowered, and she did not make any attempts at conversation; when Richard tried to talk to her, she would only answer in monosyllables. He was no more successful with the other guests, among whom he tried to mingle, and when his eyes occasionally met Mary's, they both shrugged and looked at each other in amused consternation. At one stage Ruchira disappeared from the room and, going out to look for her, Richard found her in Mary's bedroom, sitting on the edge of Mary's bed, her hands in her lap and staring sulkily at the wall. She didn't stir when he came in. 'What's the matter?' he said.

She gave, though so lightly as to be almost imperceptible, that upward toss of the head and downward twist of the mouth with which Indian women express displeasure and contempt.

'You want a drink or something?'

'When you have finished enjoying your friend's party,' she said, 'I'm ready to go home.'

'Now what's this?' he said and sat down beside her and laid his arm round her shoulders. At once she jerked forward, hissing, 'Don't touch me.'

'You're being absolutely silly.' He succeeded in sounding English and cool, but he didn't feel that way. Her perfume pervaded Mary's bookish bedroom, her gold necklace, set with rubies and pearls, sparkled round her neck. He had to check a desire to get down on the floor and bury his face in her pale rose lap.

'All right, so I'm silly, but please take me home.'

He looked at her quizzically, one eyebrow raised, the way he had looked at other, earlier girl-friends when he had been displeased with them. This made her drop her haughty manner and say, 'It's such a horrible party, why did you bring me here – I'm bored, there's no one to speak with —'

'I'm here. Mary's here.'

'Mary!'

'You said you liked her.'

'Why should I like her? She is only an old maid. And all those awful people she has asked to her party – no one like that would ever be invited to *our* house, and if Mummy knew you made me meet such people —' He took her hands, but she snatched them away and cried, 'I suppose she thinks I'm not good enough for her English friends!'

He was appalled. There was such a large-scale misunderstanding here that he didn't know where to start clearing it up. He tried not only that evening but for several days afterwards, never with any success: Ruchira was not interested in listening to explanations, she didn't want to be reasoned with. She would listen only to the promptings of her own heart, and these were too strong to be affected by anything he might have to say. She was immensely proud, immensely intolerant, utterly unfair. And he loved her all the more for it, for being so strong and unreasonable, like some force of nature, a monsoon storm or a tiger in a jungle. How insipid by comparison were the pleasures to be derived from talking with Mary, even though they did agree on so many things and had the same sense of humour. Ruchira had no sense of humour at all – or rather, a very simple one, she thought it funny when people fell down or bumped their heads – but it didn't matter to him. When they were together, he laughed differently, not with her but always at her, out of a deep delight with the way she was.

He saw less and less of Mary, indeed of everyone he had known hitherto, and was not as meticulous in the performance of his duties as he ought to have been. All he wanted was to be with Ruchira, and when he couldn't be with her, he preferred to be alone to think about her, to read, study, listen to Indian music on records. He became quite knowledgeable about certain aspects of India – could, for instance, talk intelligently on the various exponents of Bharata Natyam or the differences between Shankaracharya's and Ramanuja's commentaries on the Vedanta Sutras – and he liked to spread all this new information before Ruchira who was impressed and nodded at everything he said and contributed, 'Yes, we have a very ancient culture, many foreigners like Max Müller have come to study our philosophy.' Then he laughed and tried to kiss her, whereupon she pushed him away and jumped up, the time for being serious was over and she cried, 'Come on, let's go!' and ran to sit in his car. Often nowadays she made him take her out dancing – she had been taught by her brothers and danced supremely well, but he couldn't do much more than walk her stiffly round the floor. She had a lot of fun laughing at him and trying to teach him, and she loved being there with him in a crowded restaurant. He liked it too, although the food was dreadful, and so was the interior decoration, and the band very loud and not always in tune. But the floor was packed with gay young Indians, all of them superb dancers, their supple bodies twisting and shaking, and the girls had all kicked off their shoes and were lightly dancing on slim brown feet.

Sometimes, when they were at her house for too long and he didn't take her out anywhere, Ruchira became very melancholy. She would sit on the swinging sofa, holding on to one of its ropes and leaning her head against her arm, pushing herself with her feet into gentle, lazy motion. She would look out into the garden, at the prize chrysanthemums, the rose-creepers, the pigeons, and the butterflies, but without taking pleasure in anything she saw. At such times she didn't care for him to share the swing with her, so he would be sitting on the top step of the veranda, looking up at her and waiting for her to become more responsive. From time to time Ruchira's mother would call some question out of the drawing-room, where she was drinking her unending cups of tea, and sometimes her face would peer out at them through the french windows, looking worried between the two long swinging diamond earrings; and Ruchira would say irritably, 'We're all *right*,' and the Princess would withdraw, and Ruchira's feet gave an angry push to the swing which made it go to and fro in irritable jerks.

On one such occasion, when her mother had withdrawn, Ruchira burst out – 'I'm so tired of it, why can't she leave me *alone*', and hid her face against the arm holding the rope of the swing.

Richard didn't say anything, but continued sitting on the step of the veranda in a sympathetic attitude.

'I thought when I left college everything would be different, I'd been so looking forward to this time, and now it's the same, the same, the same every day!' She was wearing a garland of jasmine blossoms in her hair and, impatient to be fiddling with something, she took it off and tied it round her wrist instead. 'I thought I was going to do such a lot,' she said as she tied, 'I was going to visit so many places, different countries, and meet people . . .'

'Ruchi?' called the Princess from inside.

'Yes, yes, yes!'

'All right,' the Princess said mildly and probably poured herself another cup of tea.

Richard said, 'Why don't you marry me, and then you can go to all sorts of places with me?'

After a short pause she said, 'You're only saying it because you feel sorry for me.'

'No,' he said, 'as a matter of fact I've been thinking of it for ages.'

This was not strictly true. He had not thought of himself as getting married, he enjoyed being by himself and had intended to stay like that for some years to come. His feelings for Ruchira were, he thought, too *different* to mix them up with thoughts of marriage, and although he had sometimes wondered how he would be able to part from her when the time came for him to be posted to some other country, to think of taking her away with him seemed no more realistic than to think of taking away India itself. She belonged here. Nowhere else was good enough for her, no other country, indeed no other city but this one of ruins and gardens and fantastic moonlit nights. He would not only not have dared but even not have wanted to remove her from her setting.

There was, however, as he ought to have known, nothing she wanted more. Although she did not commit herself on that first day when he asked her, nor on subsequent occasions when they returned to the subject – and she often returned to it – she was certainly very interested in all he might have to offer her in exchange for what she had. The idea of being a foreign diplomat's wife pleased her, and she had many questions to ask, such as where he might expect to be posted next, and whether one had to give and go to very many parties, and how long it would be before he expected to be a full ambassador. Her questions made him laugh, and she herself made him laugh too – the way she did not in the least pretend to care for him but only for what he could offer her. He teased her about it, became mock plaintive and asked, 'And me?' 'Oh you,' she said and tossed her head, 'who cares about you?' But she put her hands on his shoulders and looked into his face with deep, promising eyes, so that he felt that afterwards, when he had satisfied all her conditions and she had allowed him to marry her, then she would love him. The thought of that excited him so much that he felt he must do everything she wanted: for now he had forgotten about not intending to get married and was only afraid that he would lose her. And for fear of that he dared not admit to her what had been becoming more and more clear to him for the past year – that he was not cut out to be a diplomat, and would never do well. Before he and Ruchira had started talking about the future together, he had in fact already half decided to leave the service and had toyed with all sorts of other delightful possibilities. He would return to Cambridge and study anthropology, or take a teaching job in America, or live cheaply in Spain. Now he could no longer think about these things but, for her sake, had to pretend to himself that he liked it where he was and that one day he would become an ambassador and she – how distinguished a figure she would make! – an ambassadress.

He began to take her to those cocktail parties and receptions which to him were an unpleasant duty but to her a promised land. And at once, from the very first one he took her to, he realized that she had been right and he wrong. This was the stranger because the first party was what, left to himself, he would have regarded as a particularly dreary one. It was given by one of the trade commissioners, a red-faced man with a redfaced wife, whom Richard and Mary had always considered as exceptionally dull and colonial. Their house was furnished in conventional English style but with those few Indian touches (carved Kashmiri tables and papiermâché cigarette boxes decorated with Moghul horsemen in turbans) which were nowadays obligatory as part of the new policy of cultural contact. The guests were most of them very much like the hosts, which was not surprising since they did the same kind of job, lived in the same way, had had the same education, and talked with the same accent about the same things (transfers and postings, house rent allowance, children's schooling). Everyone not only sounded but even looked rather alike, especially the women who all wore ill-fitting dresses made out of shimmering Indian silks that had been meant for better things.

Ruchira, however, was enchanted: by the place, the people, the party, everything. She wore a brocade sari, and its myriad-coloured threads were caught in the light now as pink and now as gold. Her eyes sparkled, she smiled so expectantly that her fellow-guests, who were not usually attentive to strangers, smiled back at her, showing their bad English teeth, and they talked to her about the weather and the merits of various hill stations. She met them more than half-way, was prepared to hold conversation on any subject they presented to her, matched platitude for platitude, but bubbling with such spirits, such vivacity, her face so full of happiness that, while her lips moved and spoke one thing, what she was actually saying was something quite different: *O brave new world that has such people in it!* And so impressed was she by the manner in which everyone spoke that her voice too began to change, and to the best of her ability she too spoke flat phrases in flat English accents. She mentioned to several people how much her father had enjoyed his years at Oxford; she ate sausages, olives, dainty canapés; she drank sherry; once, when no one was looking, she squeezed Richard's hand and then burst out laughing while her eyes moved impatiently round the room to see who next would come up and make conversation with her.

The only parties she refused to go to were farewells for Mary, who was posted back to England just about this time. Nor did she want Richard to go to them, which meant that he saw nothing of Mary until about two days before her departure, when he managed to get to her flat. Most of her furniture had already gone, and she was in the process of packing up the rest of her belongings, helped by several of her young men who were eagerly scrabbling among packing-cases and little heaps of discarded goods. Mary was busy – she seemed to be the only one seriously packing – but she found time to sit with Richard for a moment on two remaining chairs in a corner of the room. Out of habit he looked round to see whether there were any interesting new books he could borrow from her, but of course there weren't; everything had gone, the shelves were empty.

She didn't reproach him, not even jokingly, for having dropped her so abruptly, but she did ask him quite soon why she had never been allowed to meet Ruchira again. Richard looked a bit embarrassed, and she said, 'It was that awful party, wasn't it?' and without waiting for him to confirm this went on, 'I never seem to be able to do anything right here, you know? There's always some misunderstanding.'

One of the young men showed her a corkscrew, broken but with a decorative wooden head to it, and, eyes modestly lowered, asked her what to do with it.

'Oh just chuck it away,' she said absently, and turned back to Richard: 'In some ways I'm actually glad I'm going.'

'It is to be thrown away?' the young man asked her. Suddenly he lifted his bashfully lowered eyes, and they were radiant with hope as they looked at her: 'Can I take it away?'

'But it's *broken*, Rajee.' Nevertheless he bore it off, gazing at it in love and triumph; and, for the rest of Richard's stay, young men came up bearing useless objects that they asked for permission to take away.

'It isn't that I didn't like it here,' Mary said. 'But it's been so ridiculous – I mean, here was I doing my absolute utmost not to be the English lady from the High Commission, only to find that that's precisely why I'm made friends with: not because I'm Mary, with lots of liberal ideas and unconventional attitudes, no, but because I've got duty-free liquor and the latest records . . .'

'So what,' Richard said.

'So nothing, but it's humiliating to be loved only for what one values least – one's broken corkscrews —'

'What's it matter,' Richard said, 'what you're loved for, as long as you *are*?' And intercepting a surprised look from Mary, he went on, quite fiercely: 'Why the hell should anyone love us for ourselves? We're not all that bloody marvellous, are we?'

She didn't answer, in fact she suddenly remembered that she was in the middle of her packing. She got up and attempted to close a suitcase, and all the young men sat on it to help her. They laughed and kicked their legs in the air and had a lot of fun and jokes.

After he left Mary, Richard drove straight to Ruchira's house. They were due to go to the Flag Day celebration at the Swedish Embassy. Ruchira wasn't quite ready yet – it always took her hours to get ready for these parties – so he sat in the garden to wait for her. It was very still in the garden, and warm and full of scents; the moon was bright silver. Once Ruchira leaned out of her lighted upstairs window and called down to him, 'Won't be a sec!' She was brushing her hair and wearing her white and silver sari, which he thought of as her moonlight sari. He wished they didn't have to go but could sit here in white wicker armchairs and play cards and perhaps listen to music. Some of the trees in the garden were squat and round, others tall and pointed, but all were black and absolutely still as if they weren't trees at all but something painted or cut out against the sky which shone like silver paper. Richard thought of a miniature he had once seen: a lady and her lover reclining on cushions; it was night but fountains sparkled, flowers bloomed, girl musicians played on viols, and far and shadowy in the distance a city slept, amid dark hills and trees. The lady's breasts were uncovered and hung about with pearls that gleamed in the moonlight. Richard shut his eyes and didn't know whether the too sweet scent of night flowers that assailed him and made him languorous came from the garden or from his memory of the miniature.

Ruchira, shimmering in her white and silver, moved lightly across the lawn, full of energy and impatient to be off. He held out his hand to her and, when she failed to take it, touched her wrist. 'Don't you know you're supposed to stand up for a lady?' she said. 'Anyway, stop lounging, it's late.'

'Sit with me for a minute,' he pleaded in a lazy voice.

'It's late,' she repeated, but she sat down – not so much, it turned out, to oblige him as to be able to readjust the bracelet on her wrist. 'I hate to be late,' she said as she did this. 'I mean, half an hour is all right, you're supposed to be late by half an hour but not more, that's rude *and* you miss all the fun. There's something wrong with the catch,' she said and imperiously held out her arm to him; he began to fiddle with the bracelet. 'Carol Bennett is going to be there, I have to see her and fix up about Thursday morning at the pool. I like Carol, she's nice — Oh, I suppose you think only your Mary is nice with her fat legs and all those books she has. Everybody likes reading and books and all that, but good heavens what is the use of making a fetish out of it the way she does. I mean, first you have to live, isn't it, how can you know about anything unless you've actually lived? Haven't you finished with that yet? You are slow.'

'I think there's a screw missing.'

'I think you have a screw missing.' She laughed at her joke, throwing back her head, her teeth gleamed, her laughter was high, girlish, and clear. 'Oh leave it, never mind.'

She took the bracelet off and stuffed it into his pocket. 'And don't forget to give it back,' she said and slapped him playfully on the cheek. 'Ready? Well, you look *almost* all right. Mummy, we're going!' she called, and when there was no answer – 'I suppose she's in her bath, when she is not drinking tea then she is having a bath, that's my poor mother. Give me the keys, I'll drive. No, I want to – you drive so slowly, let's get some zip into her. I can't understand why you have that car anyway, why don't you have one of those snappy sports models like that Italian's, what's his name? By the way, did I tell you he has asked me to play tennis with him? Shall I?' she said, slow and teasing. 'Shall I, Richard? . . Well, you tell me, what am I to do, when you can't play tennis properly, or dance, or anything, naturally I have to find other people who can do these things. When you're such an awful dud.'

However, in spite of these derogatory words, she put out her hand and tousled his hair. Encouraged, he tried to hold her, but she slipped away from him and ran to the car and had started it before he could catch up with her. In fact, she drove it off for a little way down the road and then stopped and watched him running after her. She leaned out of the window and laughed out loud at him in her high-spirited way.

The Biography

Jonathan Jones, having come to India to collect material for a biography of a great dead leader, found himself before long involved in a peculiar way with that leader's niece. Anita had, in fact, been more than only niece: the leader was unmarried, and she, his closest relative, had been companion, confidante, hostess to him. She was well fitted for this latter role especially. A tall, handsome woman, she lent tone to any assembly, and although her manner tended to be somewhat sulky and phlegmatic, that only gave her an additional stateliness. She was indeed in every way born to move among the great ones of this earth, and, thanks to her distinguished uncle, she did. After his death, however, things changed for her.

She was the first and most important person Jonathan approached in his quest for biographical material. He was nervous of her at first, for she was so very distinguished, so very stately, had moved in such high worlds; but she received him graciously, and after a time became more than gracious, became positively forthcoming and was, day in day out, very lavish with the time she devoted to him. He was delighted with and grateful for this generosity of hers, but as the weeks wore on, he began to feel that it was not she who was being so generous with her time but he with his. They talked about – or rather, she talked about – many things which were not connected with his subject of study at all, and instead of dwelling on the uncle, Jonathan found that she just as often dwelled upon the niece. She also frequently repeated herself and told him things in great detail which she had already told him before, simply because, he guessed, it gave her pleasure to recall them (the banquet in Moscow, the trip up the Rhine with champagne and two ex-kings). And sometimes, when he tried to tell her that he was not coming on a particular day, she would almost force him to do so by rapid promises of searching out some special manuscript for him, or by recollecting a forgotten treasure-trove of photographs to be sorted out on the very day of his absence.

She need not have been lonely. She was still a person of distinction, and many people sought her out. The trouble was, she did not care for most of them, they did not come up to her standard. Only occasionally she would take a liking to someone, the way she had to Jonathan – strangely enough, almost always to a foreigner. For her own fellow-Indians she had little time to spare. As she often enough told Jonathan, 'Things have changed nowadays', and whenever she used this phrase, she sighed and ran fastidious fingers over her hair at the back, and her fine eyes were melancholy.

Besides Jonathan, her special friend at the moment was an Englishwoman, Miss Bridget Law, who had come to India in order to write a book on The New Woman (*From Purdah to Parliament* it was to be called). Anita liked to have both her friends, Jonathan and Bridget, together with her in a cosy three-some, and she often invited them to meals which were exquisitely cooked and served. Unfortunately they were always marred for Jonathan by the presence of Bridget, whom he did not care for at all. Everything about her offended him – her constant talking, her coquettish ways, her large teeth – but what he hated most was the way she flattered Anita, grossly, constantly, and Anita taking all this flattery as her natural due and without batting an eyelid.

'Anita dear, I know you'll think I'm quite, quite batty, but I was looking at some miniatures today – do you know that the Kishangarh Radha is the image, the absolute image of you?' She turned to Jonathan: 'Do you remember the picture? The nose' – she held her hand by the side of Anita's nose, and Anita obligingly modelled it in profile – 'and the forehead, and the long cut of the eyes. The complete image.'

Anita looked down with a little smile and said, 'And what about my grey hair?'

'Show me one,' Bridget demanded. 'I think it's marvellous, raven-black – look at me now,' she said and lowered her head and plucked with both hands at her hair. 'Ah well,' she sighed, 'we can't all have the gift of eternal youth, can we, Jonathan?'

'I wouldn't know,' said Jonathan crossly; he was indeed, at twenty-eight, at least ten years younger than either of them. He scowled down into his plate. He always felt on such occasions that he too was expected to add his mite of flattery – in fact, there always occurred at some point a tiny waiting pause; when he showed no indication of intending to fill it, Bridget would say, 'These men', and give a conspiratorial smile at Anita who, however, could not help looking a little bit disappointed.

Yet Anita was not an unintelligent woman, and there were many things about her that Jonathan liked and respected. Sometimes she spoke about the past in a passionate way that was really stirring and brought the subject of his study as glowingly alive to Jonathan as he could wish. She loved those old days, those old glories, and when she spoke of them, she sat up straight with her fine shoulders squared and her eyes shining and a smile of triumph on her sulky lips. It was not only the grand social occasions that she remembered but also the all-night meetings, the diplomatic crises, the political manœuvring, opponents outwitted or won over: her uncle's world that he had ruled over and dominated for years, so that now that he was gone, it was impossible to imagine it still going on without him. She resented the fact that it did. None of the present-day leaders was worthy to be his successor and, as she often said, though they strutted and made much of themselves now, when he was alive they would not have dared as much as raise their eyes to his face.

'She must have been terribly in love with him,' Bridget opined to Jonathan.

He had not asked for her opinion and did not want it; nor did he want her company, but of this too she seemed oblivious. Unfortunately they lived in the same hotel, and she had developed the bad habit of dropping into his room and making herself quite at home there while engaging him in intimate chat.

'I suppose that's why she never got married,' she said. 'There just wasn't anyone to match up to him. What do you call it – an *uncle*-complex?'

She laughed at her joke, but Jonathan didn't. He wouldn't have minded discussing Anita with someone else, but not with Bridget who so often partook of her hospitality together with him and always on such occasions was full of fulsome praise.

'What do you think of her?' Bridget said.

'I like her.'

'Oh of course – so do I – I *adore* her. But you don't feel she's a little bit inclined to —'

'Excuse me,' Jonathan said coldly and, lifting the receiver off his telephone, made one or two calls. Bridget didn't mind; she waited, and meanwhile strolled through his room and riffled through his papers. As soon as he had finished, she said:

'I always feel she's a bit too inclined to live in the past. Why isn't she in Parliament? Why isn't she doing things?

Instead of just thinking about her uncle. I mean – let the dead bury their dead and all that.'

'Why tell me? Tell her.'

'I will,' Bridget said. 'Certainly. She needs her friends to wake her up.'

And really one evening, when they had all three had one of Anita's exquisite meals and now sat on her lawn enjoying the cool night air, Bridget began to broach the subject. Not too openly, as she had done when she was alone with Jonathan, but in an oblique, almost insidious way, with many smiles and side-glances at Anita. She always talked to Anita in this way, like a courtier, testing her reactions as she went along – all the time, on the one hand, fearing to offend her and, on the other, hoping to say something that she would want to hear.

'The country *needs* you,' Bridget said. 'A person of your experience and judgement, how many are there? No, not one.'

Anita shrugged sullenly. She wasn't shrugging off the compliment – she knew without having to be told that there was no one who could match her experience and judgement – but she was shrugging off the country. They didn't deserve her, not the way they were now.

'You should be right there in the Cabinet,' Bridget said. 'Advising them, guiding them, the way *he* did.'

'I can't deal with those people. If you knew what they were like —' Her eyes flashed with contempt. She began to tell them about the Ministers, she had a derogatory anecdote about each one of them: how one had disgraced himself at a state banquet by his dirty eating habits, another had squandered public funds in a Paris night club, a third had made crude advances to the wife of a visiting dignitary . . . She grew more and more heated, and was quite unlike her usual stately self as she dwelled on the shortcomings of the country's leaders. Jonathan was uncomfortable – he felt she was perhaps saying more than she meant, and certainly more than he should listen to – but Bridget was being very sympathetic, and clicked her tongue, and led her into further and further indiscretions: until at last she stopped as if recollecting herself, and there was an awkward pause, and Jonathan got up and said it was getting late and time he went.

Everything she had said left him feeling very uneasy. Probably she was right, and the people she had spoken about were in many ways crude, vulgar, even corrupt. But it seemed to him that these politicians had to be judged not by the usual standards but in relation to what they were and where they came from – in relation to their villages, their caste, their communities, the poverty and superstition embedded in the soil from which they sprang. Seen like that they appeared in a different light, and now it was not they who were strange and wrong but Anita herself. Moreover, and worse, Jonathan began to have his doubts about her uncle too. When he thought of the dead leader as the world knew him and as Anita described him – with his English tastes and education, his elegant profile, his dreamer's eyes, his fine sensitive nature, his fastidiousness, his fondness for quoting Shakespeare and Lewis Carroll: when he thought of all that, Jonathan wondered again and again, could he have been like that and yet, at the same time, his country's – *this* country's – leader? Jonathan realized that it would have been easier if he had stayed at home in England and done researches in records and through personal interviews with visiting Indians. But having come here, having walked the Indian streets, had his senses battered by Indian smells, been accosted by beggars and lepers, cheated by shopkeepers, assailed by intestinal disorders – he no longer felt really qualified to make a balanced estimate of his subject. One could not, after all, tear the man out of his context, nor should one even think of him apart from it. Yet how to think of him within it, and at the same time identify him with Anita's uncle of whose grace and sophistication she spoke with bated breath?

The next time he went to see her, Anita began speaking to him in quite a different vein, and so promptly that it looked as if she had been waiting for him to come and had everything she wanted to say to him all ready and prepared in her mind. She spoke about her uncle's feelings for India, which were also her own, how intensely he had loved the country and its people, and had felt as close a bond with the simplest peasants as with the Oxford-educated intellectuals of his own class. And she herself too felt that way – yes, her uncle had taught her to love the humble people of this land, and also the land itself in all its glory with its mountains and rivers and forests. Jonathan felt as if she were deliberately giving him copy for his book, and also perhaps hoping to correct any bad impression she might have given him the last time.

She rang the bell for tea to be brought in. And then, over the cucumber sandwiches and the lemon sponge cake, she suddenly became melancholy. She confessed to him that, in spite of the great love and reverence she felt for her country, it was not always easy for her to live here. She had been educated a great deal abroad, in Switzerland and in England, and had learned to think in many ways like the inhabitants of those countries; so that when she was at home it was difficult for her to have a complete sense of identity with her fellow-countrymen who had not, as she had, learned to live a Western-style life and to love European music, painting, and literature. That was why she so much enjoyed his, Jonathan's, company, and Bridget's too, because they had the same *values* as she had, and she could talk to them without constraint about the things she held dear. Again Jonathan felt uncomfortable, because he could not return this sentiment – unless she was giving him concrete information about her uncle, he really did not enjoy her company at all, and in fact when she started talking about the things she held dear, such as European music, art, and literature, he often had to repress a yawn, and everything she said on this subject seemed strange and remote to him and quite different from anything he knew.

Jonathan had several interviews with one of the leader's former associates, who was now in his own right a very powerful Government Minister. This man was immensely busy and important. He appeared to carry on his life in public, and whatever talk Jonathan might have with him, he had to resign himself to having it before a whole assembly of secretaries, journalists, petitioners, hangers-on. Actually, Jonathan did not gather very much information here. The Minister, though he had worked closely with the dead leader, did not choose to be very forthcoming about him but restricted himself to eulogies of the highest order. Probably he meant them – he owed reverence to the leader not only because he was dead but also because he had been his elder and guide – but, in any case, they served as an effective smoke-screen against any more personal revelations. Nevertheless, Jonathan kept coming back. The truth was, he enjoyed it here and found the atmosphere stimulating. There was a general excitement in the air, a feeling of being at the heart of things, with a constant stream of visitors and of rumours and news. Yet in the middle of all this activity the Minister himself, who was the cause of it, remained as stonily placid as some large holy idol. Jonathan found him fascinating. He was a grossly ugly man, squat, fat, and baldheaded, always dressed in flimsy white muslin which did nothing to hide his flabbiness; but he had the physical confidence that good-looking people usually possess and which was probably in his case the result of the constant adulation that surrounded him. He was slow in his movements, his voice was pitched low, and everything he said was delivered in a throwaway manner which, while suggesting that he did not care who listened and who didn't, forced his audience to be constantly on the alert. His personal manners were atrocious – he scratched himself when and where he felt like it, frequently burped, and had altogether no inhibitions of any kind; but at the same time he had a sort of courtly courtesy which was quite different from Western courtesy and fitted in well with the fluent but somewhat bizarre English in which he spoke to Jonathan.

Anita hated him. He symbolized for her, more than any of the others, the change that had come over the leadership of the country since her uncle's day. Whenever she met him – at one of the public functions or receptions she occasionally attended – she treated him with abrupt discourtesy. Jonathan once witnessed a meeting between them. It was at one of those interminable functions organized to felicitate someone on some achievement and took place in a large marquee filled with hired chairs. A platform had been improvised at one end, and on this sat several of the organizers, the guest of honour – an ex-Governor just returned from foreign tour, his stout figure hung about with garlands – and the Minister. The Minister too had been garlanded, but he had taken these tributes off when he got up to make his speech. There were a lot of speeches, and they were all very long. Anita, elegant in a natural-coloured sari of tussore silk, was in the front row, which consisted not of chairs but of sofas specially hired for the comfort of the more important guests. After the speeches, tea was served from long tables set with little saucers on which were arranged fritters, nuts, and coloured sweetmeats. As always when food was in the offing, there was a rather unseemly scramble around these refreshments, but the more important people did not have to participate in this because their plates were handed to them where they sat. People came up to Anita to greet her, folding their hands to her respectfully, and many more clustered round the Minister and with even greater respect. But suddenly the Minister made his way out of his surrounding circle and jumped down from the platform. Considering his bulky body, he did this with really remarkable agility. Smiling broadly, hands folded in greeting, his Congress cap set jauntily on his bald head, he advanced towards Anita. She did not rise to meet him but merely inclined her head in a stately manner. People gathered round them, keeping a respectful distance and smiling happily to witness this meeting between two great ones.

'What pleasure and joy to see you here,' said the Minister in his courtly way. Anita turned her face in order to do something dainty to her hair at the back.

'We don't see enough of you nowadays,' said the Minister.

With her face still averted, Anita replied, 'Things have changed,' very shortly and cryptically and in such a way that, if he had chosen, he could have taken offence.

But he did not choose at all. He remained as hearty as before, only now, instead of addressing himself directly to her, he spoke more towards the people standing round and took the opportunity to make some highly complimentary references to her uncle. Everyone nodded at this, and he said more on the same subject, so that it became almost a speech addressed to the bystanders who gathered closer round him in order not to miss a word; and surrounded by this circle, he moved away, quite easily and naturally, drawing many people after him, including some of those who had before been paying court to Anita.

She raged about this for days. Bridget, who had not been present but had been told all about it, was equally indignant and said scathing things about the new type of politician. Jonathan, however, refused to contribute anything. Feeling both of them glance at him expectantly, he tightened his lips and looked away from them with a closed, obstinate expression on his face. So the next time they were alone together, Anita found it necessary to explain the situation to him. She was calm and patient with him. She said that her one endeavour, ever since she had got to know him and had learned of his project, had been to try and make him understand the different forces at work. Her uncle had stood for enlightenment, liberalism, progress in the Western sense; but the new politicians who had succeeded him understood nothing of these ideas, for they were uneducated and had had no contact with other, more advanced cultures. As a result the country was now in danger of slipping back into that benighted state of self-centred ignorance from which her uncle had worked so hard to rescue it. She quoted from one of his speeches: '*We must keep our doors and windows open and let the fresh breath of knowledge blow in from other lands*. But they've shut them!' she suddenly cried, as if in pain.

Jonathan said as gently as he could, 'But is that necessarily bad, would you say? I'd have thought there were two sides to it.'

There was a moment's shocked silence and then she said, 'Everything I've told you, all these *weeks* I've spent trying to make you see our country and our problems – it's all been a waste. You still don't understand.' She shut her eyes and, putting back her head, laid her hand on her fine full throat in a gesture of anguish. She stayed like that for a while, and Jonathan looked at her and felt exasperated.

She pulled herself together. She opened her eyes and even managed to smile at him. 'No,' she said in a stirringly calm voice, 'let's try again. Let's start again, shall we? It's so important for you to know who he was, what he was, everything he stood for. Only then can your book even begin to do justice to him.'

'Oh my book,' said Jonathan. 'I'm afraid I've rather given up on that.'

'What do you mean?'

'I really don't think I'm fit to write it. As you say – I don't understand.'

'But that's why *I*'m here!' she exclaimed. 'To explain, to help you! Please don't be shy with me. I *want* to help you. Your work has become mine too.' She got up and began to stride up and down the Persian carpet. Her sari rustled and swished, her jewellery gently jingled; her strides were graceful yet strong and full of purpose. She clasped and unclasped her hands. 'We must write about him in such a way that the world will understand what he was and what those are who call themselves his successors.' She stood still before him and her eyes were brilliant with excitement: 'I long to start – direct me, treat me only as your assistant! I'm ready.'

She threw herself into the work heart and soul. She even began to do some writing of her own, putting down her recollections of her uncle as best she could – which was not very good for, as she herself admitted, she did not have much practice at composition. She wrote in a round, rather charming schoolgirl hand, and her style too was stiff as a schoolgirl's: 'One day Uncle was called to the door he went and there was a policeman there. Uncle was very much disturbed.' She watched him while he read, biting her lip, and when he had finished, she said shyly, 'Is it all right?' She saw him hesitating, cried, 'Oh I know – it's awful!' and suddenly snatched the sheets from his hand and tore them up. 'If only I could give you some idea . . .' she said passionately, pressing her hand against her heart as if to prevent it from bursting with all its unexpressed contents. But actually the process of trying to put her thoughts down in words did seem to release something in her, so that afterwards she was always more poignant, more nostalgic in her recollections than ever before.

Visiting the Minister became for Jonathan almost an antidote against being with Anita. He no longer pretended that he visited him in quest of information, but came purely in order to be there: and the Minister accepted this, as he accepted the presence of so many others, and was always glad to see him. Indeed, he appeared to take quite a liking to Jonathan and even invited him to come and see him early in the mornings, at five or six, when there were few people with him and he had time to talk. It was not an hour to which Jonathan was very much accustomed, but he was always glad when he had made the effort, for at that time it was very peaceful in the Minister's house. The Minister too was peaceful; it was after his morning prayers, and he sat on a mat on his veranda and ate his breakfast. He ate crudely and with relish and was served by a pockmarked servant-boy in torn clothes. Sometimes from behind the screen doors came the sound of women's voices – the Minister was said to have many daughters, as well as sheltering various widowed sisters – but none of these women ever appeared, for the family was what was known as old-fashioned and the women kept to the inner rooms.

Sometimes, on such mornings, the Minister would talk to Jonathan about his early days. His father had been a village carpenter, but he had died when the Minister was seven years old, and then they had all moved into the care of an uncle who carried on the same trade in a near-by town. The uncle had a large family of his own to keep, and there was not always enough to eat for everybody. Nevertheless, the Minister spoke with tenderness and affection of those days: about his mother who often pretended not to be hungry so that her children could be given her share, or about the school he attended run by an idealistic furniture-maker who taught them nothing but Urdu and arithmetic. He also recalled his beginnings in politics and his early meetings with the dead leader. The first time he had gone to the great man's house, he had shuffled off his shoes at the entrance and had been overawed by all the splendid furnishing. The leader had been kind and charming and made him feel at his ease: but when it was time to leave, he had seen a servant looking with such contempt at his shoes standing on the threshold that he had become shamefully aware of how cracked and ugly they were. He laughed, remembering this, and shook his head at himself.

'And the niece?' Jonathan asked.

'Oh the Memsahib!' said the Minister with another laugh. 'Yes, I was always very frightened of the Memsahib. How grand she was! In her presence I did not dare raise my eyes from the ground . . .' He became thoughtful and then – perhaps because it was so early in the morning and the cares of the day had not yet properly begun – he became more outspoken than he had yet been: 'They were so different from us, these people. Even our language they could not speak properly. When he gave a speech in English, it sounded wonderful, but in Hindi – sometimes we wanted to laugh. But at that time who cared about Hindi? It was only for common people like us.' He paused for a moment and thoughtfully scratched the back of his fat neck. 'Yes, we admired him greatly – he was our leader, our guide, our guru – but now that he is gone, it is easier for us. We can do things our own way.' Then he added: 'Sometimes I feel sorry for the Memsahib. This is not a country for Memsahibs any more, but where else can she go? She is here, she hates us, she suffers. What to do? It is history.' He shrugged, and gave a healthy burp to digest his breakfast.

As if in reproach of Jonathan's idleness, Bridget began work on her book (*From Purdah to Parliament*). She did so in full public view, sitting in the lounge of her hotel surrounded by sheaves of foolscap paper and tapping away like mad on a tiny typewriter perched on her knees. In the evenings she came to Anita's house and treated her to a reading of the day's work:

'Indian womanhood has really come into its own in these last decades. Now there are not only legions of women doctors, lawyers, and even engineers, but Woman has also penetrated into the hallowed halls of parliamentary government. But while she may be called "modern" in the best possible sense of that word, she has remained first and foremost "a Woman". She has not given up one whit of her femininity, and the busiest doctor or legislator may be seen going about her demanding tasks enveloped in the graceful folds of the traditional sari.'

At first Anita listened with great interest, and when Bridget asked for her opinion, they held discussions on what had been read. Bridget scribbled busy little notes in the margin, and then she gathered up all the sheets and cried from out of a full heart how fortunate she was to have the benefit of Anita's knowledge and experience to guide her; and finally, in gratitude, she pressed her lips to the other's cheek, while Anita accepted this tribute with closed eyes and a suffering expression. After some time, however, as the readings went on and on, fulsome in praise of the Indian woman and her exalted status, Anita fell silent and, when pressed for her opinion, merely shrugged and looked into the distance and her sulky mouth became sulkier.

It was to Jonathan that she first expressed her doubts. She said that Bridget meant well, and that it was good to have such books published abroad in order to give the world a favourable image of India's progress – and then she sighed, and fell silent, and studied her shapely hands. It was true, she began again after a while, the emancipation and complete equality of women had been one of her uncle's most cherished ideals, and there *were* women doctors and lawyers and Members of Parliament – 'And yet,' she said hesitantly, and Jonathan agreed with her and said, 'The child-brides and the widows.'

'Yes,' said Anita but absently, so that it was clear she was not thinking of them; and then she broke out: 'Look at me, I'm emancipated, I'm educated —' Quite unexpectedly, her eyes filled with tears. She turned aside her face to wipe them away; as she did so, she smiled ruefully and said, 'Why don't you write *my* biography?' and for a moment Jonathan wished he could.

The Young Couple

Cathy was thrilled at going back to India with Naraian, her new husband. They had many ideas about the things Naraian would do for his country once he got back there, and all their English friends envied them because of the challenge, the life of purpose, that awaited them.

On arrival, Naraian wasted no time in looking round for a job in which his skills would be properly harnessed in the service of his country. Early every morning he went out to make his contacts, leaving Cathy behind in the new flat they had rented. They had a glorious view from their flat: on one side of all the neighbouring houses, they could look right down into courtyard after courtyard and see what everyone was doing; and on the other side of a decadent, eighteenth-century mausoleum, very large, very ornate, with a vast dome which looked especially magnificent against the sunset. The flat had been got for them through an uncle's influence, and they were very happy with it, even though it was small and up on the roof and very hot because of the sun beating down on it all day.

In the mornings, after Naraian had gone, Cathy wandered by herself through their two rooms and out on to the roof in her flimsy nylon nightie, yawning and plaiting and unplaiting her long blonde hair. Sometimes she looked down into the courtyards, to see men shaving, servants lighting fires, sometimes at the birds wheeling round and round the dome of the mausoleum. So early in the mornings everything was still pastel coloured – the sky a pale washed blue, the trees a misty green – all the things that later would become violent and hot. Cathy ate a bit, read a bit, let the hours slip happily by till she saw Naraian again. Some time during the morning the sweeper-woman came to clean – thin, cheerful, tattered but gaudy, with big silver anklets and very white pointed teeth; there was no other language but smiles and nods by which she and Cathy could communicate so they made what they could of those. Actually, the sweeper-woman swept very badly indeed, but since they seemed to have established such friendly relations, Cathy felt shy to point this out to her, though Naraian sometimes did (rather too rudely and loudly, Cathy thought, but the sweeper-woman never seemed to mind, on the contrary, she showed her pointed teeth wider, whiter than ever).

In the evenings Cathy usually met Naraian in town somewhere. They visited a lot of restaurants, patronizing one for its South Indian food, another for its ovenbaked chickens, a third for the band and the dance-floor. Everywhere they met friends – Naraian's friends, with whom he had gone to school and college and had sat about with in restaurants before he had left for England. All of them were restless and discontented, like Naraian himself, and they swore at the Government, at the social set-up, at their families, at the poverty and backwardness of the country. Some of them had jobs, found for them usually through the influence of some relative, others were like Naraian still looking for jobs and meanwhile living at the expense of their families who, it appeared, kept them very well for they were all expensively dressed and seemed to have plenty of pocket-money to spend in restaurants, cinemas, and record-shops.

Although in England Cathy had enjoyed parties and company, here she always preferred to be alone with Naraian. She didn't care for these friends of his, she thought they were silly and spoiled; and besides, or rather most of all, what galled her was their attitude to herself. It was true, they were polite to her, but the trouble was they were *too* polite, in a very formal and courtly way, so that she felt all the time that her presence was a strain on them and they would have been happier without her. Moreover, they treated her – as the wife of a friend – with such undue respect, always looking shyly away from her, never raising their eyes to her face, that she, who was young, blonde and pretty, felt slighted; especially as she knew how fervidly interested they were in women and saw how they nudged each other and their eyes became moist and dreamy whenever any passable young woman hove into sight.

Naraian, on the other hand, loved being with his friends and quite often seemed to forget that Cathy was there with him. She was rather a demonstrative girl and liked kissing and holding hands with Naraian when other people were looking, and indeed in England he had enjoyed that too, and they had sat in coffee bars and on park benches with their arms slung closely round each other. But here, when they were in public places, Naraian took care to see that there was a decent few inches of space always between them, and that their hands never for a moment, not even by accident, as much as touched. Nor did he talk to her much when they were out together or let his eyes stray in her direction: yet he was always, she noticed, very much aware of what she was up to, for if for instance her dress had crept up over her knee or a button had come undone, he was quick to notice and by indirect means – such as clearing of throat or significant glances somewhere in her direction if never directly at her – managed to draw her attention to such accidental immodesties.

Alone at home, however, he was as affectionate with her as he had always been and (perhaps it was something in the climate?) even more passionate. They spent a lot of time lying on their beds or walking round the hot rooms stark naked together. This was very pleasant indeed. They could both afford to be seen uncovered, for she was a tender unflawed white, delightfully plump where necessary, full of curves and grace; and he pale brown, spare, hard, and muscular, not tall but beautifully put together. They were both very young, with all their strength still intact in them. No wonder then that, when there were only the two of them together, they were always completely happy.

Unfortunately – or so it seemed to Cathy – there were not only his friends but his family too. It was not that his family were not happy with Cathy: they were, they enjoyed having an English daughter-in-law, they were proud of her. When Naraian had first brought her, they had made a splendid wedding for them, with hundreds of guests, revolving neon lights, fireworks, two bands, and several days of over-eating. Nor had they raised any objections to the young couple living separately, although the family house was quite large enough to absorb a number of married sons with their young families: on the contrary, they had even helped them find this flat and pay a year's advance rent on it. The father liked to wink in a tolerant, expansive way at business friends while remarking that young people – well, one had to understand, they liked to be alone, none of the old fogies around them; and the mother, too, explained that this was the way it was in modern times, young to young and old to old, that was the trend nowadays, large joint families were really quite out of fashion. Still, of course, they expected to see quite a bit of the young couple, and the original idea had been that they should come to the two main meals at the family house. As the mother said, where was the sense in running two kitchens, and besides, what did poor Cathy know about our Indian preparations of which his mother knew Naraian to be so fond? But two large heavy Indian meals a day proved too much for Cathy – and, after his years in England, for Naraian too – and very soon they missed out on one of them and after a while on both of them, so that in the end they found themselves going only on Sundays and on special festive occasions.

Cathy did not enjoy these obligatory Sunday lunches. First of all they always had to parry some resentment, especially from the mother, who made a mouth for the first half-hour and thereafter when she remembered, and remarked that she was glad the food at home was still good enough for them at least once in the week. There were also comments from her on Naraian's appearance which, she liked to hint, indicated severe under-feeding, and these merged, like the chimes of a clock, into whatever else was said during the afternoon. But it wasn't only what was said or hinted which disturbed Cathy and made her wish they could spend their Sundays in some other way: there was also a certain heaviness about the house that weighed on her and made her feel oppressed, sleepy, liverish. This heaviness was physical – it was in the too rich, too abundant food, in the solid ornate pieces of furniture, in the silver, the waist-high vases, the brocade curtains, the carpets, the giant plumped-out cushions; and in the people themselves, the mother, large, handsome, with a proud bosom draped in shimmering silk and adorned with a great deal of golden jewellery, the father, also large, comfortable, good humoured, very fond of his food and proud of his house and all his possessions, among whom he liked to number Naraian and blonde English Cathy.

She could not complain that they did not care for her. The trouble was they cared too much, so that she felt herself lapped around and drowning in more love than she had ever before, among her cool English family and friends, encountered. Everything that she and Naraian said or did, the way they looked, everything was the subject of scrupulous family concern, to be pointed out, discussed, wondered at and advised over. Not only by the parents themselves but by all other members of the family – of whom there were so many that sometimes Cathy was no longer sure who they were or whether she had met them before at all. Quite a few of them lived in the house, and the rest dropped in throughout the day, staying for meals or eating quantities of sweets and nuts in between meals, while their cars were lined up in the drive outside with their chauffeurs squatting under the big banyan tree and enjoying a surreptitious game of cards.

What the family discussed most vigorously was Naraian's refusal to enter any of the family business concerns or to accept any of the jobs which they kept arranging for him. They took this up with him over and over again, every Sunday, and often – in fact, usually – the discussions turned into a quarrel, with voices raised, tables thumped, and once or twice it had ended with Naraian, and Cathy in tow, storming angrily out of the house. All the way home, and indeed for days afterwards, he fumed indignantly against his own family in particular and against Indian families in general, who would not allow a man to take his own decisions but regarded it as their right to take them for him. Cathy heartily supported his indignation and hoped that now he would do something decisive and independent to face the family with next Sunday; but all that happened was that he discussed the whole thing with his friends who, of course, had plenty of similar complaints of their own, and so they all chimed together on one of their favourite subjects – the tyranny of family domination – and next Sunday the whole thing was repeated with identical words of anger and perhaps with Naraian storming out of the house again.

Of course, it was not easy to do anything decisive and independent while they were living the way they were, with Naraian's family supporting them completely; and the most important step now was for Naraian to get himself a job to support the two of them. But, as they both fully agreed, it was no use rushing anything; he had to have time to look around and weigh possibilities, so that in the end he would have something beautiful and useful where he would be fully engaged. In the meantime, Cathy would have been glad to help out and get a job herself. She had done quite a lot of things in England, she had been a receptionist to a Harley Street specialist, a sales assistant in an airlines office, once for a brief while a waitress in a coffee bar, but of course she realized that it was impossible to do anything like that here because of her, or rather the family's, background and social standing. The sort of jobs this background and social standing permitted her she was not qualified to do. Nevertheless, often nowadays, after Naraian had gone out, she lay on the bed, on her stomach, one foot with a silver slipper dangling from it up in the air, her fingers twisting and untwisting the end of her golden plait, and read the Situations Vacant columns in the newspapers. It was depressing: there was nothing, nothing at all for her. It was all either for readers and senior lecturers in sociology, or for fitters and mill-inspectors preferably with experience in small-grind machines. Soon her eyes involuntarily slipped to the matrimonial columns, which amused her. But she felt frustrated.

Also, perhaps, a little bored and lonely. She met plenty of people but they were all Naraian's friends or his family, so that she began to feel almost as if they were forming a ring round her out of which she could not break. She confided this impression to Naraian, who scorned it. She was free, he insisted, to do exactly as she liked, go wherever she wanted. But where was she to go, what was there to do? She never liked to go anywhere without Naraian, and there was certainly no question of walking freely down the road: she was stared at, sometimes mocked for being white and different, certainly always an object of attention. Sometimes, when it seemed to her that she was getting a complex about this, she decided to brave the stares and taunts and go by herself into the city bazaar. Actually, it wasn't so bad: she drew a lot of attention but she ignored it. She pretended to merge with the crowd of modestly veiled women, sick cows, pickpockets, and obtrusive hawkers. When she got home, she was breathless but quite excited. She spread her purchases on the bed with a feeling of triumph: they were invariably things she didn't need – a red velvet purse sewn over with silver spangles, green and gold sandals, a picture of a swan reflected in a lake which was made out of a piece of mirror – but she was proud and pleased with herself for having gone out to buy them.

One Sunday, at lunch with Naraian's family, she was questioned about these excursions of hers. It seemed she had been seen (one was always seen, there were so many relatives, so many acquaintances, so much time in which to pass the word around) and what had excited particular comment was that she had been alone and on foot. 'Where is the need?' said Naraian's mother. 'One word, and I shall come myself with the car to take you.' This was true: Naraian's mother, sisters, sisters-in-law, always eager to go out shopping in a car, frequently urged her to join them. But she had enjoyed herself more on her own. She looked for help to Naraian, but he was busy eating a mango; either he hadn't heard, or he didn't want to get involved. She would have welcomed a word from him to tell his family about the independence customarily enjoyed as a right by English girls.

No such word coming, Naraian's mother drove her point home further: 'Our girls don't go into these bazaars alone. It is not proper for us.'

There was a waiting pause. Cathy knew she was now expected to make a tart reply which would instigate her mother-in-law to an even tarter one, after which it would be her turn again, and so on until they had got a really good family row going. But Cathy didn't say anything. Unlike the others, she had no liking for these family rows. Instead she looked again towards Naraian who was now busy eating the flesh round the stone of his mango, always a delicate operation calling for all one's concentration and skill. Cathy lowered her head, lifted the napkin from her lap, and folded it several times very neatly. She sensed disappointment in the air, as if she had let everyone down.

But it was she who felt let down. That night, after an hour or two of sleeplessness, she woke Naraian up quite roughly: 'You could have said something,' she said. 'Instead of sitting there with that damn mango.'

She knew at once, though it was dark and she couldn't see his face, that he had caught on. Perhaps he had been harbouring a bad conscience. But all he said was, 'What's the matter with you? In the middle of the night.' He yawned and tried to go back to sleep. But she turned on the light.

'Throwing me to the wolves,' she grumbled.

He blinked against the light, but sat up. His chest and shoulders were naked, smooth, and brown.

'You could have *said* something.'

'What? What could I have said?' He put one arm round her; she was wearing a low-cut pink nylon nightie with a lace top, and her blonde hair hung loose about her shoulders. She leaned against him: 'I felt so awful. As if they were all going to attack me or something.'

'Silly girl.' He drew her closer against himself, kissed her hair. She felt comforted and soothed.

'The way she was carrying on,' she said, with a pout now that she felt she had an ally, even though a belated one. 'Really, I mean, what had I *done*? I hope it's not a crime to go out, is it?' And when he didn't say anything, she gave him a jab and looked sharply up at him: 'Well, *is* it?'

He uttered an uneasy laugh: 'Crime, crime – how you talk, Cathy.'

She freed herself from his arm and shouted: 'I could have hit you! The way you sat there sucking that mango!'

Then he became prim, his lips were narrow and his nostrils pinched: 'Perhaps she was not as wrong as you think'; and when she said nothing, only stared at him in shocked unbelief, he became even more righteous: 'It's not Oxford Street, you know. You can't just saunter down the road as you please.' He looked at her out of the corner of his eye, then decided to be bold: turned out the light, and lay on his other side to go back to sleep. He was waiting but there was no sign from her, so soon he really was asleep again.

She continued to spend her days as she had done before – padding round the flat on naked feet, stretching, yawning, plaiting and unplaiting her hair; but whereas before she had felt time lapping deliciously round her in endless honeyed hours, now her feelings were ones of boredom. The endless hours were harsh not honeyed now. When she sank down on her bed, it was not in enjoyment, soft, languid, stretching herself, but in a dry boredom with nothing to do, nothing to think, and many hours yet till it was time to meet Naraian. And even when she did meet him – she was bored with the restaurants now, she knew all the bearers down to the stains on each one's uniform, had eaten all the dishes on the menu and found them all tasting the same, the band was no longer a gay, slick group called the Merry Macs but a collection of tired men who lived in a room above the restaurant and worried about their next engagement. And Naraian and his friends still sat there, eating, drinking, smoking, condemning everything as it was now but looking forward to a future when each one had his desires and the world would be moulded by such as they.

Cathy and Naraian began to bicker. Naraian complained about the way she kept the flat – he said everything was dirty and untidy, he stumbled over pieces of discarded underwear, and where once he would have tenderly picked them up and even perhaps pressed them to his lips, now he kicked them aside impatiently, at the same time shouting at her to point out her neglect. He also shouted at the sweeper-woman more often than ever, and when Cathy interfered, he turned on her instead and soon they would be shouting at each other, while it was the sweeper-woman who tried to calm them by pursing her lips and cooing sweet words into the air, as if she were soothing two ruffled pet birds in a cage.

Not for pleasure so much as in defiance, Cathy went out more frequently by herself. She visited the city bazaar several times, although there was nothing she wanted to buy and it was hot, crowded, full of smells most of which were unpleasant, and sly men with dirty fingers touched her surreptitiously from out of the crowd. Once or twice she sat on a public bus and went far out to some place of historical interest, some ruined tower or palace or mosque, and here she was happy for a while amid green grass, old stone, and silence: although what she always looked forward to most was going back home and telling Naraian where she had been. At first he used to protest, would even try and forbid her from taking these solitary excursions, but she was ready for him, opposed him with such spirit, such defiance, such *enjoyment*, that he had to retreat. But then a reaction would set in for her, and she would be sad at her victory – or rather, at his defeat. She did not like to see him overcome, even by herself, and when he turned away and said do what you like in a resigned voice, she flung herself round his neck and kissed his face all over, crying at the same time, 'If you don't want me to, I won't, I won't', and they clung together, whispered together, and soon they were lying on their bed together, fervently forgiving each other.

Always somewhat confused about dates, it took Cathy longer than it should have done to find out she was pregnant. From then on a big fuss was made of her. The family priest performed various ceremonies, and her mother-in-law and sisters-in-law took her to the best doctor. Many special dishes were cooked for her, she was exhorted to take great quantities of milk, food, and rest, and generally to pamper herself in every possible way. This she did. She spent most of her time sitting at the window of their flat looking out. Sometimes she looked out at the left side, into all the neighbouring courtyards; but what she liked best was to look out at the right side, at the mausoleum, to see the birds wheeling round its dome, and the tops of trees with the leaves looking very green, young, and tender against the weathered stone, and the sky a brilliant blue the whole day long until it faded away at dusk. She sat there hour after hour, her cheek supported on her hand. She looked forward to having a baby, to the future, to Naraian having a job and doing wonderful things. She was glad to be young and married to Naraian. 'Her cup of happiness was full,' she kept repeating to herself, it chimed in her head like a tune, she turned it over and over and smiled at it. She slept a lot, a delicious drowsiness stealing over her like kisses from a god; she stopped going out, even in the evenings when she was usually too tired to go and meet Naraian. Instead he would come home earlier, leaving his friends behind in the restaurant, and he would always bring something for her to eat for which she had expressed a liking, although there was plenty of food for her sent over from his father's house. If she was asleep, he woke her up and supported her in bed and fed her, bite by bite, and kissed the top of her head in satisfaction while she ate. If he found clothes strewn about the place, he picked them up and folded them, moving very softly so as not to disturb her.

All the week she felt fine, never better, but on Sunday mornings she always woke up sick. In between vomits, she kept saying, 'I can't go.' He said soothingly, 'You'll feel better in a minute.' Both of them knew she wouldn't, but both of them also knew that they would have to go. Naraian's father always sent a car for them. The car-ride made her feel worse than ever, but when she arrived at the house, the mother and the other ladies in the house and the female servants smiled triumphantly to see her in this state. Yes, they said, that was the way it was in pregnancy (and they all of them knew all about pregnancy), no use complaining, one just had to put up with it. And anyway, they added, nodding approvingly at her queasiness, it was a healthy sign, and they pinched her cheek and patted her and found her altogether to their satisfaction. But she couldn't bear them near her with their smell of hair-oil, perspiration, and rich food – a smell indeed that pervaded the whole house till she felt it would drive her mad and she had to rush out into the garden. But here too she felt oppressed in the same way as she did in the house, for the smells from the creepers and the flowers were too rich, and the flowers themselves, fed with too much fertilizer, too thick and fleshy.

One Sunday there was a surprise for her. It was a more than usually crowded Sunday, with a lot of uncles present, and there was evidently much to discuss. Naraian too was part of the discussion, in fact, he seemed to be the centre of it, and she glanced over at him wondering what was going on, and once or twice he glanced back at her with a hint, she thought, of uneasiness. But everyone else seemed to be pleased, the father smoked a fat cigar and smiled complacently round it, and the mother too was smiling, she was very tender with Cathy, patted and fondled her hands, saying, 'Now everything will be nice for you.' And an aunt said, 'Such a fine salary too, it is a great chance for him,' whereupon the mother retorted, with a trace of sharpness in her voice, 'Naturally, a clever boy like that, five years in England, it is his due.' Cathy caught Naraian's eye again; he looked away quickly. She was very miserable; she shut her eyes but she couldn't shut out the sense of this large, well-fed family with Naraian and herself trapped in the middle of them.

But she should have been glad, not miserable. What was she complaining about? he asked her, as soon as they were home again. At last he had a job, and moreover a well-paid one, and now they could be as independent as she had always wanted them to be. She shook her head: she couldn't or wouldn't put her feelings about this job into words. 'It has a lot of scope,' he urged and looked at her anxiously, and when she refused to respond, he took on a defiant little swagger: 'You don't get a salary like that every day.' Cathy began to cry; very quietly tears rolled down her cheeks. Seeing these, he lost his temper, he shouted 'You're mad!' but there was pain in his voice, for he too was disappointed that finally, after all the tall talk, he should have ended up with a job in his uncle's firm. She tried to stop crying but she couldn't, the tears came faster and faster, nor did she have a handkerchief to wipe them with, so that she had to do so on her bare arm, burying her face in it and making dirty tear-streaks all down her cheeks. Her nose too had begun to run. In anger and disgust, he drew a handkerchief out of his pocket and threw it at her and she took it gratefully; she tried to explain to him, tried to disguise the cause of her tears now that she saw so clearly that he too was hurt, but she was too far gone to be able to speak coherently, and instead of words deep sobs rose out of her chest. He turned away from her, left the room, the flat, banging the door behind him, and in despair she heard his footsteps running away from her down the stone staircase.

As it happened, however, he enjoyed his job. He sat in an air-conditioned office all day, had a peon to himself and a share in a secretary, attended board meetings, and entertained at business lunches. He came home in the evenings, tired but satisfied, and took pleasure in telling her his day's doings. They rarely went out in the evenings now. It was no longer necessary to visit any restaurants, for his mother had put a cook in the kitchen who prepared meals almost as rich as those in the family-house. This cook took all his orders from the mother-in-law, who indeed had given him instructions not to bother Cathy because of her delicate state. This suited Cathy very well; in any case, she hardly partook of any of his preparations but fed herself on cream crackers and bars of chocolate. The cook quarrelled a lot with the sweeper-woman, and the mother-in-law, who came at least once every day, participated in these quarrels. Altogether she took a great interest in everything that happened in the flat and poked around in the cupboards and even under the bed to see what went on there. She found a lot of things amiss, in fact, almost everything. The flat and its shortcomings now became the chief topic of discussion at the Sunday meals.

Cathy shut her ears to it, as much as she could. She would not be drawn. She heard how the flat was uncomfortable, unsanitary, an unnecessary expense – and those stairs! For a woman in her condition! She kept quiet: she knew that, among these adepts, she would always be outwitted in argument – or rather, shouted down, which counted as the same thing. But it irked her that Naraian did not come to the defence of their nest as vigorously as she felt he might have done. He parried the thrusts now and again but, it was to be noticed, half-heartedly, so that the mother was always left in clear possession of the field. There were no more rousing family rows the way there had been when it had been a question of Naraian's taking a job; no more banging of doors, storming out of the house with Cathy in tow, the two of them brave young champions against the combined mass and power of the rest of the family. Now, Cathy felt, no one was against anyone; it was as if they had joined forces.

And indeed, Cathy was beginning to notice more and more that Naraian was himself dissatisfied with their home. Apart from complaining about the way it was kept, he complained about the place itself too: it was hot, the construction was cheap, the whitewash flaked off the walls, the stairs were dark, narrow, and dangerous, the water did not rise properly into the taps. All this was true but it hadn't mattered to them before, they had been so proud to have a place of their own. He didn't seem to remember that; or perhaps it was a part of his life that he had outgrown the way he had outgrown some other things too. For instance, he no longer roamed naked round the flat with Cathy, and, when she did it, he told her not to. He also seemed to have outgrown all the friends with whom he had sat in restaurants. He hardly ever went to meet them now. Sometimes she asked him why not, and then he made a face to show that they were no longer quite good enough for him. She was sorry. She hadn't liked them and yet something young and nice had gone out of Naraian's life with them. And something else went out of life when one day Naraian dismissed their old sweeper-woman. Cathy was sad and wished for her back, though she could not complain that the woman's dismissal had put her to any inconvenience, for the very next day Naraian's mother sent another sweeper whom she had trained herself to clean in corners and to use Vim.

At the same time a large bedroom and dressing-room were being got ready for them in the family-house. Everyone tried to keep it secret from Cathy, but it was all done with such glee – a great deal of whispering always went on, and Naraian was beckoned into the room, and there were winks and veiled allusions – that her suspicions were soon aroused. When at home she confronted Naraian with these, he tried to hedge and say it was only if they wanted to stay over weekends or take naps on Sunday afternoons. Soon, however, he was speaking out more clearly and he said, did she think he was going to put up with a place like this for ever? and he kicked a door so that its poor, cheap wood splintered a bit further. And the only thing Cathy could think of in defence was, but look at the view! and pointed towards the dome of the mausoleum darkening against a tender flush of sunset and a formation of birds, wings a-tilt, going round it swift as bats in a last flight before plunging down into the trees to settle themselves to sleep.

In reply, Naraian pulled a contemptuous face which made it clear what sort of importance he attached to the view. But this expression – though an honest, spontaneous one – he held for only a moment; the next he had corrected it, looked in fact sympathetic. Probably he had recollected the way they had once used to talk, the art galleries they had visited in England, the plays they had witnessed, the opinions they had so seriously held on life and how to live it.

'What does it matter, Cathy,' he said, putting his arm round her, and his voice was tender, and so was the way he looked at her, 'what does it matter *where* we are as long as we are together?'

They kissed. This kiss was delicious but, even while it was going on and set within it as in a heartshaped frame, she had a vision of the room that was being got ready for them: the same heavy, shiny furniture as the rest of the house, a carpet, ample satin bedspreads matching the curtains.

Passion

Apart from the fact that they had both been in India for about a year and both had well-paid jobs with British cultural organizations, Christine and Betsy had very little in common. Nevertheless they shared a flat. Their friends – Christine's friends especially, Betsy didn't have all that many – were surprised when they first decided on this step and wondered how it would ever work out; but in fact it worked very well, perhaps just because they were so different, and led different lives, and so never got in each other's way.

The mantelpiece in their flat was always full of invitations, and they were almost all Christine's. She was tall, slim, and good-looking. She had a number of Indian boy-friends, who would call for her at the flat in the evenings in order to take her out in their cars. Sometimes she wasn't quite ready and she would trill from out of the bathroom that she wouldn't be a second; Betsy in the meantime invited them to make themselves comfortable in the sitting-room and have a drink. Sometimes they had several before Christine finally appeared, and then they jumped smartly to their feet while she, laughing and breathless and tying a gauze scarf round her hair, flippantly apologized for keeping them waiting.

Her favourite escort was a tall, handsome officer of the President's bodyguard called Captain Manohar Singh ('Manny' to his friends). Betsy too was glad when it was Manny who was taking Christine out, and the longer he was kept waiting the better Betsy liked it. She felt good sitting next to the handsome Manny on the sofa and talking to him. She talked to him about India – Indian philosophy or music, or about the current political situation – while he drank one whisky after the other and sat at his ease with his large legs apart and a good-natured, listening expression on his face. Betsy sometimes had reason to believe that he wasn't really listening, for he never made any kind of remark that could be construed as a comment on what she was telling him. Indeed, he hardly said anything at all, and when he did, it was something completely unexpected like, 'Boy, did we have a party last night! Wow!' But for Betsy it was really enough to be allowed to talk to him and look at him at such close quarters to her heart's content. Manny was a Sikh, and he had an exquisitely barbered, shining black beard and wore a dark blue turban; his eyes were not dark but surprisingly light-coloured, a pellucid grey shining like a lake between the heavy fringe of his black lashes.

Once Manny kissed Betsy. It was entirely unexpected. They were sitting on the sofa and Betsy was telling him about her preference for the Kangra school of painting over that of Basohli, when suddenly he jumped on her. Really, there was no other word for it – he *jumped*, took a leap from where he was sitting and snatched her into his arms. She gave a short cry of shock, but next moment his lips were pressed weightily on hers, his tongue – strong, pulsing, muscled like some animal alive in its own right – pushed its way into her mouth; beneath his silk shirt she could feel his chest and his ribs as strong as steel. Waves of rapture passed over her like a fainting fit. But it seemed he was more collected than she was. As suddenly as he had seized her, he pushed her away, hastily adjusted his turban and got to his feet as Christine came breezing in, wafting scent and shouting 'Darling!' 'Darling!' he answered with his great boom of a laugh. 'Again you are late, ho-ho, darling!' He was quite unembarrassed, while Betsy was left sitting stunned on the sofa with her hair dishevelled and her skirt slipped high up on her thighs.

With few friends and few entertainments, Betsy had very little to do in her spare time and spent most of it reading. She often went to the American library and became well known to the local staff there. One member of the staff was particularly assiduous in finding the books she wanted and keeping back those she had asked for. He was a slim, shy young Indian who, like a thousand other clerks, was always dressed in a clean but rather old white shirt and Western-style trousers. In the evenings, when she took a taxi home from the office, Betsy often saw him standing in a bus queue. The queue was always immensely long, and many of the buses that passed were crowded and did not even stop. He looked very patient standing there, holding a small, worn brass tiffin-carrier in his hand. Once it was raining, and she saw him trying to protect himself by placing the tiffin-carrier on his head. She stopped her taxi and offered him a lift; he got in without a word.

'Where can I drop you?' she asked.

'Where you are going.'

'But that may be miles out of your way.'

'It is all right.'

That was all she could get out of him: 'It is all right.' For the rest, he sat straight and silent on the edge of the seat, holding his arms close to his sides; he was very wet and exuded vapours of dampness and discomfort. When the taxi stopped at her house and she got out, he got out with her, without a word. 'Do you live near here?' she asked; she felt quite guilty about him by this time. 'It is all right,' he said, and stood and waited. Perhaps he was waiting to be asked up, but Betsy couldn't do that because Christine was having people in. She fumbled in her bag for her keys and, in the process, feeling nervous and hurried, dropped many things on the pavement. He stooped to pick them up, and she cried out in alarm, 'No, don't bother!' She crouched down with him on the pavement, and they both scrabbled for her things and got wet in the rain. When she had found her keys, she stuffed everything back into her bag and tucked it bulging under her arm and ran inside, leaving him standing. She had a bad conscience about him for hours afterwards.

A few days later she passed him again at the bus stand. Feeling embarrassed, she looked quickly the other way, but he had seen her, and without a moment's hesitation he ran into the road and signalled her taxi to a halt; he waved both arms like a person in distress. But he wasn't in distress at all, he only wanted a ride with her. Again he came to her door and stood there, waiting expectantly. When she asked him up, he agreed at once. He sat down on a chair and looked round him with undisguised curiosity, up and down the walls, across the ceiling, at all the furniture. Betsy said, 'Would you like a drink?' Now that she had brought him here, she didn't know what to do with him.

When she had mixed him his drink, he held the glass as if it were some strange object and then he asked: 'It is alcohol?'

'Oh dear.' She bit her lip and stared at him in consternation. 'Don't you drink? I'm so sorry —'

But he took a big gulp and, after coughing a bit, another; then he finished the glass. She looked at him apprehensively. 'It doesn't taste very nice,' he said.

'No, if you're not used to it. It never occurred to me that you might not – everybody seems to drink such a lot. I mean, all the people one meets —' She stopped herself, for she realized she was saying he was not the sort of person one met. She sought desperately for something to say to cancel this out. But he did not seem to have noticed. He was smiling: 'It is a funny taste.'

'Would you like some more?'

'Yes.'

This time too he drank it down very quickly, as if it were water or tea. She would have liked to warn him but was afraid of hurting his feelings. When he had finished, he was smiling again; he seemed happy.

'Once we drank beer,' he said. 'It was at my friend's sister's wedding. We hid behind the cowshed, but afterwards one of the uncles found the empty bottle, and how angry everyone was with us!' He giggled. Betsy realized to her dismay that he was drunk. 'We were very mischievous boys. I could tell you other stories also . . . It is a nice place here. Who else lives here? There are many rooms?' He got up and began to walk round the room as if he owned it. He picked up objects and asked their price, and peeped into cupboard doors. 'I think you must be getting a lot of salary. How much? More than 1,000 rupees? More? How much more? Tell me, please. Only for my information.'

Suddenly and without any warning he was sick all over the off-white rug. He stood there and retched, and held his stomach and groaned. Betsy laid her hand on his forehead. 'Don't worry,' she said. 'It doesn't matter.' She had to turn her head away, but she felt terribly sorry for him.

And afterwards she blamed herself severely. She disliked herself for having mismanaged the not overwhelmingly difficult task of inviting an unsophisticated young man up to her flat and making him welcome. She longed to make amends, to invite him again and see to it that the occasion went off with dignity on both sides. Yet at the same time she felt that she could not bear to have him here again, indeed ever to see him again; and what she would really have liked to do was to forget the whole incident and the person who had caused it.

A day or two later she heard an altercation at the door. Angry voices were raised, and then her servant came in. 'He says he wants to see you,' said the servant accusingly. The young librarian had followed him into the room, looking indignant and like a man determined to stand on his rights.

'Your servant was rude to me,' he said as soon as they were alone. He waved aside her explanation and apologies. 'I am not very much used to being treated rudely by servants.'

'Betsy!' called Christine from inside her bedroom. 'Has Manny come?'

'Not yet!'

'Who is that?' asked the young man sternly, but before Betsy could explain, Christine stood in the doorway. She was wearing a pink flowered wrap which she held shut with one hand. 'Hallo,' she told the young man.

Betsy said, 'This is —' and realized she didn't know her visitor's name. He was too stunned by Christine's appearance to help her out.

'I'm Christine,' Christine said. She waited politely for him to introduce himself, but when he didn't, she smiled at him in her friendly way and disappeared again inside. She could be heard, a moment later, singing in her bath. The young man remained staring at the spot where she had stood.

Betsy explained, 'We share this flat.' She smiled: 'I don't even know your name, how silly.'

'Har Gopal. She is English also?'

'Oh yes. She works for the British Council.' For want of anything better to say, she began to tell him about Christine's job. But he did not listen. He looked rather distraught, glancing now round the room, now at the spot where Christine had stood. Betsy noticed how refined his face was, with a delicately chiselled nose and sad eyes. Every now and again he brought his hand up to his open collar, pressing the two ends together over his throat as if wanting thereby to improve his appearance; it was a movement at once modest and self-protective. Betsy found herself feeling very tender towards this young man.

Then Manny came to fetch Christine. He was in uniform and all his buttons shone and so did his beautiful, brown, hard-leather boots. He strode up and down the room, waiting for Christine, immensely tall and exuding a smell of whisky and eau-de-Cologne. His eyes had merely swept for a second over the top of Har Gopal's head – it did not need more than that for him to sum up a fellow-countryman. With Betsy he was, as usual, absently affable. He had never, after the event, given a sign that he remembered having kissed her. Probably he didn't remember. He strode about the room, thinking of other things, and only became alert when Christine entered. She was no longer in her négligée but in a primrose-yellow dress, and golden sandals with high heels which made her even taller than she was. The room seemed very small with these two in it, and when they had gone, it seemed very empty.

Har Gopal spoke bitterly: 'Are they your friends? I don't like that Sikh. I know his type very well.' When she made no comment, he spoke harshly to her, as if she had dared to contradict him: 'I tell you I have seen hundreds like him. What do you know about it?' Neither of them in the least questioned his right to speak to her in this manner.

'I am B.A. Kurukshetra University,' he said next. 'Yes, now you are surprised. You thought I was just anyone, isn't it? B.A. in history and philosophy. And my wife is a matriculate. Come here.' He beckoned to her with his slender, fine-boned hand, displaying a surprising authority, and she went.

He jumped on her in the same sudden way Manny had done. Betsy thought, do all Indian men make love like this? In spite of his frail appearance, Har Gopal was strong. Not with Manny's massive body-strength, but he had a sort of sharp, incisive, relentless quality which rode down opposition. He went straight ahead without question, not skilful but resolute, steely. He commanded respect.

Betsy was in love with Har Gopal. If she hadn't been, the situation might have become embarrassing. He came every day to the flat, and when any of Christine's friends was there, he sat in a corner like a poor relation and looked at them with burning, hungry eyes. Afterwards he was angry with Betsy and blamed her for any lack of respect he felt had been shown to him. Christine was always very nice and tactful with him, and in return he went to some pains to make serious conversation with her. He would tell her about the unemployment problem in Uttar Pradesh, or the number of light aircraft manufactured by the Hindustan aircraft factory per year. She would appear to be listening and would say 'No really?' and 'How fascinating!' in between, without irony. She might be doing her nails, daubing on the varnish with exquisite little brush-strokes, and he would look on in fascination. He loved seeing her do her nails. Sometimes he asked Betsy why she didn't paint hers, and he clicked his tongue in disapproval when she held them out to him, clipped very short and one or two of them bitten down at the end of her short, squarish fingers.

But she took a lot of trouble for him. She brushed and brushed her hair till it shone, and then she slipped a red band round it. She wore white frilly blouses and short skirts and white ballet shoes and a gold locket round her neck. She loved going out for walks with him and would tuck her hand proudly under his arm. He allowed her to keep it there and walked by her side in a stately manner, with his head held stiffly. Many people looked at them. They were both about the same height, both short, but he was thin and she was rather stocky with very muscular legs. Once or twice they met people he knew – some friend or neighbour – and he would stop to exchange a few words in a rather formal, self-conscious way, and though her hand remained tucked under his arm, he made no attempt to introduce her. But if they met anyone she knew, some fellow-countrymen from her office or the High Commission, she made a point of introducing Har Gopal at once, flaunting him and clinging to him in such a way that her acquaintances became embarrassed and looked away and parted from her as quickly as possible. But Har Gopal always behaved correctly and said 'Very happy to meet you', and shook hands all round the way he knew foreigners did.

Betsy confided a lot in Christine. She needed to have someone to talk to about Har Gopal. 'I know it's ridiculous, ridiculous,' she said and buried her head in her arms, overwhelmed with laughter and happiness. 'He's all wrong – of course he is – *and* he's married, *and* three children.' She hid her face again and her shoulders shook laughing. She tried to but could never quite explain to Christine what it was she loved so much about Har Gopal. His finely drawn features, yes, his dark, dreaming eyes, his sadness, his sensitivity: and also – but how could she tell Christine this? – she loved the shabby clothes he wore, his badly cut cotton trousers and his frequently washed shirt with his thin wrists coming out of the buttoned cuffs. She was positively proud of the fact that he looked so much like everybody else – like hundreds and thousands of other Indian clerks going to offices every morning on the bus and coming home again with their empty tiffin-carriers in the evenings: people who worked for small salaries and supported their families and worried. She frowned with the effort of trying to express all this to Christine and said finally that well, she supposed she loved him for being so typically Indian.

Christine laughed: 'But that's why I like Manny too.'

Betsy had to admit that Manny too was typically Indian–but in a very different way. Manny was the India one read about in childhood, coloured with tigers, sunsets, and princes; but Har Gopal was *real*, he was everyday, urban, suffering India that people in the West didn't know about.

Har Gopal often asked her: 'Do you talk about me with Christine?' He wanted to know everything that they said. When she teased and wouldn't tell, he twisted her wrist or squeezed her muscles till she screamed. He loved practising these boyhood tortures on her; it was the only way he knew of being playful, for that was how he had played with his friends at school and college. He had never had a woman friend before. But he had had many male friends, and they had had grand times together. He often told Betsy about his friends, and it always put him in a good mood. He had a serious, even melancholy nature, but when he recollected his student days, he became gay and laughed at all the mad pranks they had played together. One of his friends, Chandu, had been a great joker, and how he had teased the masters at school! No one could do anything to him, because his father was an important man in town. Another friend had had the ability to chew up newspapers and even razor blades. They were all crazy about the cinema and went to see the same film over and over again till they knew the lyrics and dialogues by heart. He could still recite great chunks of old films and he did so for Betsy, and he sang the songs for her. She loved his voice, which was sweet and girlish, and the soft expression which came into his eyes when he sang; but he said no no, his voice was nothing, she should have heard Mohan, then she would have known what good singing was. They had all thought that Mohan would surely go into films and become a playback singer, but instead he had got a job in the life insurance corporation. There had been so many friends, and they had all been so close and had thought their friendship was eternal; but now Har Gopal didn't even know where most of them were. Everyone was married, like himself, and had their own worries and no more time for their friends. But he still thought about them often and wished for the old days back again, or at least to have one friend left with him in whom to confide his thoughts and have a good time together.

'Well you've got me now,' said Betsy, putting her arm round his neck, tender and comradely.

But he could not feel about her the way he did about his friends. He was, she knew, less fond of her. She excited him, and he was proud to have her, but he did not really, she often suspected, *like* her. All the loving came from her side, and he accepted it as his due but made no attempt to return it. There was something lordly, almost tyrannical in his attitude to her. When he lounged at his ease in her room, all his shyness and shabbiness – that *depressed* quality that was so evident in him when he stood with his tiffin-carrier at the bus-stop – left him completely, and he became what, as a Brahmin, he perhaps was by nature: an aristocrat for whom the goods and riches of this world were created and whose right it was to be served by others. Betsy was the one who served, and the goods and riches were the things she gave him for which he had developed a taste: English biscuits, raspberry syrup (he never again drank alcohol), tinned peaches.

He kept some clothes in her room, and when he came to her straight from the office, as he usually did, he would take off his trousers and carefully fold them and then put on his dhoti. He dressed and undressed with delicate precaution, so as never to be seen naked by any human eye, not even his own. Although his lovemaking left nothing to be desired, he never lost his reticence: his manner was always controlled and fastidious, and never for a moment was there any abandon in it. Betsy, on the other hand, was all abandon. She would fling off her clothes, leaving them just where they dropped, and walk round the room naked. Very often she forgot to lock the door, so that the servant or Christine or anyone who came to the flat could have walked in at any time. She didn't care. Her attitude shocked and at the same time pleased him. In the beginning he could only watch her undressing with his face averted and his eyes half lowered, ashamed of himself and of her, but as time went on, he looked at her boldly and with a strange smile which was perhaps partly appreciation and partly, she sometimes suspected, contempt.

He never spoke to her about his family. She wanted to know so much about them, but he always completely evaded her questions. If she insisted too much, he became annoyed and refused to speak to her at all and perhaps even went home earlier than usual. So she dared not ask much. But it tortured her to have all this area of his life concealed from her with a deliberateness which suggested she was not worthy to approach it. Why should he feel that way? He was *proud* of her – she knew he was – otherwise would he parade through the town with her on his arm and greet people he met on the way with such a superior air?

Sometimes, when she found he was relaxed and in a good mood, she tried to coax him into talking: 'Is your wife taller than me? Shorter? The same? Say!' But at once his good mood would disappear and he turned away from her, frowning. Once she asked him half jokingly, 'What's the matter? You don't think I'm good enough to hear about your family?' But at that he took on such a strange, closed expression that she realized she had stumbled on something near the truth. But she wouldn't at first believe it; she even laughed at it and said, 'My God, what am I – a fallen woman or something?' Still he made no answer, but the expression on his face did not change nor did he make any attempt to contradict or deny. She laughed again, more harshly, even though by now she felt far from laughing. It was ridiculous, something out of Victorian melodrama, but still it was true, it was the way he saw her. She felt so humiliated that she could speak nothing further and tears flowed silently from her eyes: but even as they rolled down her cheeks and her heart heaved with pain at the thought of her humiliation, at the same time – so bizarre were her feelings for him – this very humiliation actually increased, exacerbated her passion for him.

One day she went secretly to see the place where he lived. She found blocks of tenements set out side by side and surrounded by an area of waste land on which had sprung up a dusty little bazaar and a shanty colony of thatched huts. As soon as she got out of her taxi, she found herself the centre of a group of children who laughed and marvelled at her strangeness and followed her closely. She looked round her for a time, then plucked up courage and walked through the doorway that led into the compound of the first block of buildings. It was as lively here as in any street. Children played, and there were some men repairing string-beds and a number of itinerant vegetable-sellers and a fish-seller, all of whom were bargaining with women who suspiciously untied their bundles of money from the end of their saris and complained to one another about dishonest traders; other women called down from the windows that opened in tiers and rows from the tall buildings. Betsy, with her little cluster of attendant children, looked around her and did not know what to do next. Suddenly she wondered what would happen if he were to come now out of one of those dark doorways and find her standing there. She could almost see the expression of panic and fury that would instantly transform his face, and at the thought of it, she began to panic a little herself and to wish she had not come.

But then it was too late to retreat. A round little man in an English-style suit came running up to her, calling in an excited voice, 'Yes, please, yes, please! You have come to see Mr. Har Gopal?' Betsy did not recognize him, but guessed at once that he must be someone whom they had met and Har Gopal had talked to on one of their evening walks.

'This way, please,' said the little man, pushing aside all the children and leading her out of the compound. To curious bystanders he explained importantly, 'For Har Gopal in C Block.' He strutted in front while the children surged after him and Betsy found herself swept along in the procession. Behind her the women nudged and talked. The little man led her along the street and then turned into the next compound, waving a plump hand over his shoulder at her and calling, 'This way, please!'

Then she saw that the little procession had brought her back to the street where her taxi was waiting. Murmuring apologies which no one heard, she suddenly climbed into it and sat down, and the driver skilfully flicked away the children who at once surrounded the car. Betsy did not dare look out of the window, as she was driven away, and she even put her handkerchief up to her face as if she hoped thereby neither to see nor be seen.

The next time Har Gopal came to the flat he did not talk to her at all but straightaway took his dhoti and a pair of slippers and bottle of hair-oil he kept in her bedroom and, grimly determined, wrapped them up in a bundle. 'What are you doing?' she cried out in distress. He did not answer but made for the door. She clung to him to prevent him. She begged him to stay.

'Let me go, please,' he said, but standing quite still and making no effort to release himself.

'It's only that I wanted to *see* where you were.'

'You came to spy on me. Yes, and now you will laugh at me with your friends because my house is poor and I am poor.' Suddenly he shrieked: 'I don't care! You can laugh, what do I care!'

'Please don't,' she said and clung to him tighter, but he shook her off and shouted at her, 'And my position? That's nothing to you what people will say that you come openly to my home —' He sank down to sit on the edge of her bed and covered his eyes with his hands in grief and shame. And Betsy sank down beside him, and she too covered her eyes. What followed was a loud scene, echoing all over the flat, in which he spoke a lot about his position in the world and she lacerated herself with accusations regarding her own selfishness and insensitivity; and when this had gone on for a long time, and she had again and again begged his forgiveness, they were at last reconciled, and she dissolved in tears of gratitude while he was proud and gracious with her.

Then it was time for him to go home, and on his way out, they had to pass through the sitting-room where Christine sat playing ludo with Manny. Those two must have heard every word of what had passed in the other room. Christine delicately kept her eyes fixed on the ludo-board, and Manny hummed a tune to himself. Har Gopal's face took on a tight expression, and his thin body seemed to shrink as he walked through the room; he looked as he did waiting at the bus-stop. Only Betsy was entirely free from embarrassment as she ushered her lover out of the flat.

That night Christine knocked timidly on Betsy's door. Betsy was lying stark naked on her rumpled bed, reading the Katha-Upanishad. She was wearing her reading-glasses and thoughtfully twisting a lock of hair round her finger. She didn't seem to be a bit shy to be found naked. Her breasts were very much heavier than one would have expected from seeing her dressed. 'Yes, come in,' she said and shut her book with her finger inside to hold the page. 'I'm sorry, we made an awful lot of noise today, didn't we?' she said cheerfully.

Christine sat on the edge of a chair. She was wearing a flowered wrap and looked crisp and fresh and a contrast to Betsy's room which was rather untidy.

'I know it's none of my business,' said Christine, talking very quickly so as to get it over with, 'but I do think you ought to be a bit more careful.'

Betsy laughed and said, 'I wish I were the sort of person who *could* be careful.'

'Everyone's talking you know, Betsy, in the office and everywhere. I mean, good heavens, not that anyone cares about your having an Indian boy-friend – don't we all? – but he's so . . . *different* from the other Indians we all know.'

'You mean he's poor.'

'It's not that,' Christine said miserably. 'But he's – I don't know, odd. And there's something unhealthy about it all – of course it's absolutely terrible of me to be saying all this and do tell me to shut up if you want to.'

There was a moment's pause. Then Betsy said, 'It *is* unhealthy.' She tried to sound detached and dispassionate, but could not keep it up for long. 'I suppose all passion is unhealthy. Sometimes I tell you I feel *insane* – and what's more – what's terrible : I revel in it! I glory in it!' She rolled over on to her side to face Christine, and her big breasts fell to that side and her eyes shone behind her flesh-coloured glasses.

Christine was not the only person who tried to warn Betsy. One day her office chief invited her to lunch at his house, and in the kindest manner possible, full of embarrassment and apologies, told her that unless she behaved in what he called a more conventional way he would have to have her sent home. Betsy understood that he had to tell her this and that he was right, but she had no intention of changing. Instead she began to make plans what to do if she were really posted back home. Of course, she would resign immediately; she would stay and get a job locally. She was vague as to what kind of job and did not stop much to wonder whether anyone would employ her; but she knew that, whatever she did, her salary would only be a fraction of what it was now and she would have to change her whole way of life. She didn't mind that; in fact, she rather looked forward to it. She would have to move out of the flat and go somewhere much cheaper. She thought of herself in some small room in a crowded locality; to get to her, one would have to cross a courtyard and climb up a very dark, very narrow winding staircase. She would be the only European living in the house. Every day Har Gopal would come to visit her. Actually Betsy couldn't cook, but now she had visions of herself squatting over a little bucket of coal and preparing a meal for him and serving him just like an Indian wife. She might take to wearing a sari. Perhaps she would have a baby, a boy, who would grow up dark and delicate like Har Gopal.

She neglected her work in the office and was distant with her colleagues. She realized vaguely that something was going on around her and that perhaps steps were being taken against her, but she did not bother to find out what they were. Christine told her that she would be moving out of their joint flat soon; she made up some polite lies that the flat was getting too expensive for her and that she had found another smaller one elsewhere, but Betsy cut her short and said it didn't matter, that she herself would be moving out too, very soon. She already saw herself in her small room in the house with the winding staircase.

She even began to make inquiries about the rents to be paid for such places, and about how much money would be needed for the simple, Indian-style life she intended to adopt. All her thoughts were concentrated on this problem. Once, finding herself alone with Manny who was waiting for Christine to get ready, she even asked him, very seriously, 'Supposing you only eat dal and rice twice a day – how much would that come to a week?'

'Only dal and rice!' exclaimed Manny humorously. 'And what about a peg of whisky?'

'I'm being serious, Manny,' Betsy said impatiently, but it was impossible to make him be serious with her. Ever since she had started her affair with Har Gopal, Manny's attitude to her had become strange and ambivalent: on the one hand, he was rather more brusque, and even rude with her than he had been before; on the other, he indulged in sudden spurts of familiarity which extended to, whenever they found themselves alone in a room, pinching her in intimate places.

He did this now, and at the same time he joked with her: 'My two-three pegs a day I must have, otherwise I'm like my car without petrol. Hm? Han?' He encouraged her to laugh with him and drew her close, and his beard nuzzled against her cheek. She struggled to get free, but that made him hold her all the more tightly. She stared into his face, and she saw his light-coloured eyes and his red, moist, healthy mouth smiling inside his black beard. She let out a cry. He released her immediately and even gave her a push to get her farther away from him. Christine, zipping her dress, came in and said, 'Whatever's the matter?'

'It is Betsy,' said Manny. 'She thought she saw a snake.' He laughed uproariously.

Betsy did not speak to Har Gopal about her future plans. She was afraid. She knew that the idea of anyone giving up a job, an assured livelihood, was not one he would ever be able to understand. He himself was very timid about his own job and took good care never to give cause for complaint to his superiors. Not only was he very polite, even deferential, to them in their presence, but he also spoke of them in tones of the highest respect when they were not there and had no chance of ever knowing what he was saying about them. Once, when Betsy spoke with lighthearted disdain of one or two of the top people in her own organization, he rebuked her for doing so, and when she laughed at the rebuke, he frowned and became annoyed with her and said that she had no respect in her nature. The very least, he said, that one owed one's superiors was respect; and quite apart from that, one should be careful what one said about them because who knew what might not get back to them. But how *could* anything get back to them, asked Betsy, amused, when there was no one there but he and she, and surely he wasn't going to go and tell on her, was he? He refused to smile at the idea but only said that in these matters one could never be careful enough. His eyes even roved solemnly for a moment round the room – her bedroom – as if he feared someone might be be lurking somewhere listening.

One Sunday afternoon he was reclining on her bed in his rather lordly way, wearing his vest and dhoti, his feet crossed comfortably at the ankle; he had his arms folded behind his head and was staring into space with melancholy eyes. He looked noble and sensitive and gave the impression of being sunk in deep philosophic thought. This impression, however, was false, for when he finally broke his silence it was to say nothing more significant than, 'Just see, I have had this blister for two days. It is very painful.' He plaintively held up his finger to her.

She burst out laughing and, overcome with tenderness for him, threw herself on his reclining figure. 'Oh, you're so sweet, so *sweet*!' she cried, and crushed him as tight as she could as if she hoped thereby to relieve her overwhelming feelings. He cried out and struggled to get free – unsuccessfully, till she released him of her own accord. He smoothed down his hair with one hand and his dhoti with the other and said indignantly, 'How rough you are.'

She laughed again and settled herself happily on the floor, leaning her head against the edge of the bed on which he lay. She felt exquisitely comfortable and domestic and knew that this was the way she wanted her life to go on for ever. And then she blurted it out, about giving up her job and staying in India so as to be always near him.

Har Gopal was appalled. He quite genuinely thought she was mad. He argued with her, pointed out that even if she managed to get some kind of job in India, which was in itself unlikely, she would never be able to live on the salary she would be paid. But Betsy said no, she wanted to live on it; she was tired of living the way she did here, as a foreigner, as a privileged person.

'I want to live in India like an Indian,' she said, 'like everyone else, like you. Exactly like you,' and she seized his fine, frail hand and kissed it.

He drew it away from her. 'You don't know anything,' he said. 'If you had to live in a place where there is never enough water and the neighbours quarrel and you clean and clean but still the cockroaches come —'

'I don't care,' Betsy said.

'Yes, it is so easy to talk,' he said bitterly. He got up from the bed and began to get dressed, though it was not yet his usual time for departure.

'I want to give up everything for you,' Betsy said. 'To lay my whole life at your feet and say: here, take it.' She shut her eyes, carried away by the passion with which she spoke.

He uttered a short sound of impatience and turned his back on her. He began to comb his hair in the mirror. She came up behind him and put her arms round his waist and laid her cheek caressingly against his back. He continued to comb his hair very carefully; he was always careful of his appearance before going out into the street.

'I'm not "sacrificing" anything,' she said. 'Don't think that. Good heavens, what do you think I care for my job, or this flat, or money, or anything?'

He could hold himself no longer: 'No, you don't care! You are like that. You have everything in life and you throw it all away. Aren't you ashamed? There are others who would give God knows what to have something, to live nicely, but for them – no, there's nothing, not even in their dreams . . .' His voice failed him, and he could not go on. It was as if all the frustrations of his life had risen up and formed a hard ball in his chest and left him unable to speak. He waved his hand in her direction, dismissing her, not wanting her, and turned to the door.

'Don't go,' she pleaded and held on to his arm. He attempted to free himself but she held on tightly. Suddenly he became vicious. He thumped his fist on the hand holding on to his arm and cursed her in Hindi: '*Hath mat lagao, besharm kahin ki!*' He left the room, with her running after him.

Christine and Manny were having drinks in the sitting-room. Manny put down his glass and got up and strode over to Har Gopal. He seized him by the front of his shirt and shook him to and fro, and Har Gopal allowed this to be done without offering resistance. His face was frozen with fright while his body was being shaken, and the oiled, stiff hair on his head flopped up and down.

'Let him go, Manny,' Christine said in a low, embarrassed voice.

Manny gave one last shake and then flung him towards the door. Har Gopal fell down but he picked himself up again and patiently dusted off his knees and hands. Without looking back at anyone, he walked down the stairs, slowly and with dignity. Betsy followed him.

When he reached the bottom of the stairs, he told her in a tone of cold command, 'Get my things.'

'What things?'

'My things. My dhoti and my slippers, and don't forget my bottle of hair-oil.'

He stood very straight and thin and proud. But suddenly he sat down on the bottom stair. He hid his face in his arms and his shoulders shook with sobbing. She sat down next to him; she held him and murmured to him, words of the sweetest comfort.

After a while he raised his face which was smeared with tears. He cut across her murmuring and said, 'You must leave this place. I don't want you to stay with these people one day more.'

Betsy said that they would look for a place for her together; somewhere very cheap, very Indian. She glanced at him to note his reaction, but he gave no sign of having heard her and remained staring gloomily in front of him. She allowed herself to believe that his silence meant assent. At this her heart leaped in joy and her mind shone with visions of the new life that was about to begin for her.

A Spiritual Call

The river, broad, swift, swollen, was at this season too dangerous to cross in a boat. One had to walk across the bridge, which was holy and thronged with pilgrims chanting salutations as they crossed. On the other side of the bridge began a cluster of tiny temples, all of them made spruce with silver tinsel, peacock fans, gilt ornaments, and pink paint. The gods inside them were also painted pink – pink cheeks and rosebud lips – and the plump priests who looked after them were immaculately bathed and their skulls were newly-shaven and naked except for their one tuft of hair. Worshippers were constantly passing in and out to leave their offerings and obeisances, while the rest-houses, which alternated with the temples, were equally well-populated, though they offered no amenities beyond a dark, bare room of whitewashed brick. But here anyone was welcome to spread their bedding on the floor and put the children to sleep and light the cooking fires and stir in their cooking vessels, and all the time be very merry and make friends with strangers: for coming like this, here to this holy place in quest of grace, lightened the heart and made it loving to all the world.

Beyond the temples and rest-houses came a wood with a path through it; on either side of the path were trees and shrubs and sadhus doing penance. Some of the sadhus were stark naked, some wore animal skins, all had long, matted hair and beards and were immobile, so that it was easy to believe they had been sitting there for centuries, as rooted and moss-grown as the trees and as impervious as they to snakes and any wild animals there might be prowling around. Besides the sadhus, there were beggars and these were not in the least still or immobile but very lively indeed, especially if someone happened to pass by when they would set up voluble claims to alms, holding up their palms and pointing out any sores or other disfigurements that might have laid them victim.

Over everything towered the mountains, receding far up into the blue sky into unknown heights of holiness, steppe upon steppe of them and dissolved from sight at last amid mysterious white veils which may have been mist or snow or, who knew, the emanation of a promised Presence.

It was all, in short, too good to be true; a dream, though better than anything, Daphne felt, she could have dreamed of. The coolie, naked except for a loin-cloth, walked in front of her and carried her baggage on his head; he was her guide and protector who cleared a path for her through the crowd of pilgrims, warded off the beggars, and knew exactly where she wanted to go. It was quite a long walk, but Daphne was too entranced to mind; nor did she for one moment doubt that she was being led along the right way. And sure enough, her messenger, like some angel sent direct, brought her at last into the presence she had desired, for many weeks now, and when she was there and saw him again, so great was her relief and her happiness that she burst into tears.

'Welcome!' he said to her, and did ever eyes and smile swell the word with such meaning? And then he said, to her tears, 'Now what is this? What nonsense?'

'I'm silly,' she said, wiping away at her eyes but unable to check a further gush of tears.

'Yes, very silly,' he said, and turned to the others around him: 'Isn't she? A silly goose?' and all smiled at her, with him, all of them tender, friendly, saying welcome.

One or two of them she recognized, the cheerful, bearded, athletic young men in orange robes who were his permanent disciples and who had been with him in London. She did not know any of the others. They included quite a number of non-Indians, and these she guessed to be people like herself who had followed him out here to undergo an intensive course of spiritual regeneration. In addition there were many casual visitors constantly passing in and out of the room, devotees come to have a sight of him who sat for a while and then got up and went away while others took their place. Daphne was used to seeing him thus in the midst of crowds. It had been the same in London, where he had been constantly surrounded – by women mostly, rich women in smart hats who bustled round him and besieged him with requests uttered in shrill voices; and he so patient, unruffled, eating ice-cream in someone's drawing-room, and smiling on them all equally.

Nevertheless it had seemed to Daphne that his smile had in some way been special for her. There was no reason why she should think so, yet she had been convinced of it. When he looked at her, when he spoke to her (though he said nothing that he did not say to others), she felt chosen. She was not by nature a fanciful girl; on the contrary, she had always been known as straightforward and sensible, good at sick-beds, had done history at Oxford, wore tasteful, unobtrusive, English clothes. Yet after she had met Swamiji, she knew without a word being spoken that he meant her to follow him back to India. It was not an easy path. She was fond of travelling in a way and always spent her summer vacation in France or Italy, and twice she had gone to Greece: but she had never contemplated anything much farther than that. She was quite happy in London – had her few friends, her quite interesting job with a secretarial agency – and though perhaps, if opportunity had knocked that way, she would not have minded a year or two doing some sort of interesting job in America or on the continent, it was not, one would have said, in her nature to go off on a spiritual quest to India.

Everyone was indeed amazed; she herself was, but she knew it was inevitable. No one tried to stand in her way, although of course her mother – a wonderfully energetic lady of middle years prominent on several welfare committees – pointed out quite a few of the drawbacks to her enterprise. But there was nothing she could say that Daphne had not already said to herself: so that the mother, who was tolerant in the best English way and believed in people being allowed to make their own mistakes, had not spoken any further but instead confined herself to bringing forward several aged relatives who had served in India as administrators during the Raj and were thus suited to give Daphne advice on at least such basic questions as to what clothes to take and what diseases to guard against.

Everyone, whatever their private thoughts, had been too tactful outright to warn Daphne of disaster. But if they had done, how triumphantly she could, after some weeks' stay, have contradicted them! She was supremely happy in the ashram. It was not a very grand place – Swamiji had rented it for a few months for himself and his followers, and it consisted merely of three rows of rooms grouped round a courtyard. The courtyard was triangular in shape, and the apex was formed by Swamiji's room which was of course much bigger than all the others and led to a veranda with a view out over the river. The other rooms were all small and ugly, inadequately lit by skylights set so high up on the walls that no one could ever get at them to clean them; the only pieces of furniture were cheap string-cots, some of which had the string rotting away. The meals were horrible – unclean, badly cooked, and irregular – and the cooks kept running away and had to be replaced at short notice. There were many flies, which were especially noticeable at meal-times when they settled in droves on the food and on the lips of people eating it. Daphne rose, with ease, above all this; and she lived only in the beautiful moments engendered by the love they all bore to Swamiji, by the hours of meditation to which he exhorted them, the harmonious rhythm of their selfless days, and the surrounding atmosphere of this place holy for centuries and where God was presumed to be always near.

The door to Swamiji's room was kept open day and night, and people came and went. He was always the same: cheerful and serene. He sat on the floor, on a mattress covered with a cream-coloured silk cloth, and the robe he wore loosely wrapped round himself was of the same silk, and both of them were immaculate. His beard and shoulder-length hair shone in well-oiled waves, and at his feet there lay a heap of flowers among which his fingers often toyed, picking up petals and smelling them and then rubbing them to and fro. He was not a handsome man – he was short and not well-built, his features were blunt, his eyes rather small – yet there was an aura of beauty about him which may have been partly due to the flowers and the spotless, creamy, costly silk, but mostly of course to the radiance of his personality.

He was often laughing. The world seemed a gay place to him, and his enthusiasm for it infected those around him so that they also often laughed. They were very jolly together. They had many private jokes and teased each other about their little weaknesses (one person's inability to get out of bed in the mornings, another's exploits as a fly-swatter,

Swamiji's fondness for sweets). Often they sat together and just gossiped, like any group of friends, Swamiji himself taking a lively lead; any more serious talk they had was interspersed among the gossip, casually almost, and in the same tone. They were always relaxed about their quest, never over-intense: taking their cue from Swamiji himself, they spoke of things spiritual in the most matter-of-fact way – and why not: weren't they matter-of-fact? the most matter-of-fact things of all? – and hid their basic seriousness under a light, almost flippant manner.

Daphne felt completely at ease with everyone. In England, she had been rather a shy girl, had tended to be awkward with strangers and, at parties or any other such gathering, had always had difficulty in joining in. But not here. It was as if an extra layer of skin, which hitherto had kept her apart from others, had dropped from off her heart, and she felt close and affectionate towards everyone. They were a varied assortment of people, of many different nationalities: a thin boy from Sweden called Klas, two dumpy little Scottish school-teachers, from Germany a large blonde beauty in her thirties called Helga. Helga was the one Daphne shared a room with. Those dark, poky little rooms made proximity very close, and though under different circumstances Daphne might have had difficulty in adjusting to Helga, here she found it easy to be friendly with her.

Helga was, in any case, too unreserved a person herself to allow reserve to anyone else; especially not to anyone she was sharing a room with. She was loud and explicit about everything she did, expressing the most fleeting of her thoughts in words and allowing no action, however trivial, to pass without comment. Every morning on waking she would report on the quality of the sleep she had enjoyed, and thence carry on a continuous stream of commentary as she went about her tasks ('I think I need a new toothbrush.' 'These flies – I shall go mad!') In the morning it was – not a rule, the ashram had no rules, but it was an understanding that everyone should do a stretch of meditation. Somehow Helga quite often missed it, either because she got up too late, or took too long to dress, or something prevented her; and then, as soon as she went into Swamiji's room, she would make a loud confession of her omission. 'Swamiji, I have been a naughty girl again today!' she would announce in her Wagnerian voice. Swamiji smiled, enjoying her misdemeanour as much as she did, and teased her, so that she would throw her hands before her face and squeal in delight, 'Swamiji, you are not to, please, please, you are not to be horrid to me!'

Swamiji had a very simple and beautiful message to the world. It was only this: meditate; look into yourself and so, by looking, cleanse yourself; harmony and happiness will inevitably follow. This philosophy, simple as its end-product appeared to be, he had forged after many, many solitary years of thought and penance in some icy Himalayan retreat. Now he had come down into the world of men to deliver his message, planning to return to his mountain solitude as soon as his task here was achieved. It might, however, take longer than he had reckoned on, for men were stubborn and tended to be blind to Truth. But he would wait, patiently, and toil till his work was done. Certainly, it was evident that the world urgently needed his message, especially the Western world where both inner and outer harmony were in a state of complete disruption. Hence his frequent travels abroad, to England and other countries, and next he was planning a big trip to America, to California, where a group of would-be disciples eagerly awaited him. His method was to go to these places, make contacts, give lectures and informal talks, and then return with a number of disciples whom he had selected for more intensive training. He had, of course, his little nucleus of permanent disciples – those silent, bearded young men in orange robes who accompanied him everywhere and looked after his simple needs – but the people he brought with him from abroad, such as Daphne and Helga and the others, were expected to stay with him for only a limited time. During that time he trained them in methods of meditation and generally untangled their tangled souls, so that they could return home, made healthy and whole, and disseminate his teaching among their respective countrymen. In this way, the Word would spread to all corners of the earth, and to accelerate the process, he was also writing a book, called *Vital Principle of Living*, to be published in the first place in English and then to be translated into all the languages of the world.

Daphne was fortunate enough to be chosen as his secretary in this undertaking. Hitherto, she had observed, his method of writing had been very strange, not to say wonderful: he would sit there on his silken couch, surrounded by people, talk with them, laugh with them, and at the same time he would be covering, effortlessly and in a large flowing hand, sheets of paper with his writing. When he chose her as his secretary, he presented these sheets to her and told her to rewrite them in any way she wanted. 'My English is very poor, I know,' he said, which made Helga exclaim, 'Swamiji! Your English! Poor? Oh if I could only speak one tiniest bit as well, how conceited I would become!' And it was true, he did speak well: very fluently in his soft voice and with a lilting Indian accent; it was a pleasure to hear him. Daphne sometimes wondered where he could have learned to speak so well. Surely not in his mountain cave? She did not know, no one knew, where he had been or what he had done before that.

Strangely enough, when she got down to looking through his papers, she found that he had not been unduly modest. He did not write English well. When he spoke, he was clear and precise, but when he wrote, his sentences were turgid, often naïve, grammatically incorrect. And his spelling was decidedly shaky. In spite of herself, Daphne's Oxford-trained mind rose at once, as she read, in judgement; and her feelings, in face of this judgement, were ones of embarrassment, even shame for Swamiji. Yet a moment later, as she raised her burning cheeks from his incriminating manuscript, she realized that it was not for him she need be ashamed but for herself. How narrow was her mind, how tight and snug it sat in the straitjacket her education had provided for it! Her sole, pitiful criterion was conventional form, whereas what she was coming into contact with here was something so infinitely above conventional form that it could never be contained in it. And that was precisely why he had chosen her: so that she could express him (whose glory it was to be inexpressible) in words accessible to minds that lived in the same narrow confines as her own. Her limitation, she realized in all humility, had been her only recommendation.

She worked hard, and he was pleased with her and made her work harder. All day she sat by his side and took down the words which he dictated to her in between talking to his disciples and to his other numerous visitors; at night she would sit by the dim bulb in the little room she shared with Helga to write up these notes and put them into shape. Helga would be fast asleep, but if she opened her eyes for a moment, she would grumble about the light disturbing her. 'Just one minute,' Daphne would plead, but by that time

Helga had tossed her big body to its other side and, if she was still grumbling, it was only in her sleep. Very often Daphne herself did not get to sleep before three or four in the morning, and then she would be too tired to get up early enough for her meditation.

She could not take this failure as lightly as Helga took her own. When Helga boasted to Swamiji, 'Today I've been naughty again', Daphne would hang her head and keep silent, unable to confess. Once, though, Helga told on her – not in malice, but rather in an excess of good humour. Having just owned up to her own fault and been playfully scolded for it by Swamiji, she was brimming with fun and her eyes danced as she looked round for further amusement; they came to rest on Daphne, and suddenly she shot out her finger to point: 'There's another one just as bad!' and when she saw Daphne blush and turn away, rallied her gaily, 'No pretending, I saw you lie snug in bed, old lazy-bones!'

Daphne felt awkward and embarrassed and wondered what Swamiji would say: whatever it was, she dreaded it, for unlike Helga she took no pride in her shortcomings nor did she have a taste for being teased. And, of course, Swamiji knew it. Without even glancing at Daphne, he went on talking to Helga: 'If you manage to do your morning meditation three days running,' he told her, 'I shall give you a good conduct prize.' 'Swamiji! A prize! Oh lucky lucky girl I am!'

But the next time they were alone together – not really alone, of course, only comparatively so: there were just a few visitors and they sat at a respectful distance and were content with looking at and being near him – as Daphne sat cross-legged on the floor, taking dictation from him, her notebook perched on her knee, he interrupted his fluent flow of wisdom to say to her in a lower voice: 'You know that private meditation is the – how shall I say? – the foundation, the corner-stone of our whole system?'

After a short pause, she brought out, 'It was only that I was —' she had been about to say 'tired', but checked herself in time: feeling how ridiculous it would be for her to bring forward her tiredness, the fact that she had sat up working till the early hours of the morning, to him who was busy from earliest morning till latest night, talking to people and helping them and writing his book and a hundred and one things, without ever showing any sign of fatigue but always fresh and bright as a bridegroom. So she checked herself and said, 'I was lazy, that's all,' and waited, pencil poised, hoping for a resumed dictation.

'Look at me,' he said instead.

She was too surprised to do so at first, so he repeated it in a soft voice of command, and she turned her head, blushing scarlet, and lifted her eyes – and found herself looking into his. Her heart beat up high and she was full of sensations. She would have liked to look away again, but he compelled her not to.

'What's the matter?' he said softly. He took a petal from the pile of flowers lying at his feet and held it up to his nose. 'Why are you like that?' he asked. She remained silent, looking into his face. Now he was crushing the petal between his fingers, and the smell of it, pungent, over-sweet, rose into the air. 'You must relax. You must trust and love. Give,' he said and he smiled at her and his eyes brimmed with love. 'Give yourself. Be generous.' He held her for a moment longer, and then allowed her at last to look away from him; and at once he continued his dictation which she endeavoured to take down, though her hands were trembling.

After that she was no longer sure of herself. She was an honest girl and had no desire to cheat herself, any more than she would have desired to cheat anyone else. She felt now that she was here under false pretences, and that her state of elation was due not, as she had thought, to a mystic communion with some great force outside herself, but rather to her proximity to Swamiji, for whom her feelings were very much more personal than she had hitherto allowed herself to suspect. Yet even after she admitted this, the elation persisted. There was no getting away from the fact that she was happy to be there, to be near him, working with him, constantly with him: that in itself was satisfaction so entire that it filled and rounded and illumined her days. She felt herself to be like a fruit hanging on a bough, ripening in his sunshine and rich with juices from within. And so it was, not only with her, but with everyone else there too. All had come seeking something outside of themselves and their daily preoccupations, and all had found it in or through him. Daphne noticed how their faces lit up the moment they came into his presence – she noticed it with Klas, a very fair, rather unattractive boy with thin lips and thin hair and pink-rimmed eyes; and the two Scottish schoolteachers, dumpy, dowdy little women who, before meeting Swamiji, had long since given up any expectations they might ever have had – all of them bloomed under his smile, his caressing gaze, his constant good humour. 'Life,' he once dictated to Daphne, 'is a fountain of joy from which the lips must learn to drink with relish as is also taught by our sages from the olden times.' (She rewrote this later.) He was the fountain of joy from which they all drank with relish.

She was working too hard, and though she would never have admitted it, he was quick to notice. One day, though she sat there ready with notebook and pencil, he said, 'Off with you for a walk.' Her protests were in vain. Not only did he insist, but he even instructed her for how long she was to walk and in what direction. 'And when you come back,' he said, 'I want to see roses in your cheeks.' So dutifully she walked and where he had told her to: this was away from the populated areas, from the throng of pilgrims and sadhus, out into a little wilderness where there was nothing except rocky ledges and shrubs and, here and there, small piles of faded bricks where once some building scheme had been begun and soon abandoned. But she did not look around her much; she was only concerned with reckoning the time he had told her to walk, and then getting back quickly to the ashram, to this room, to sit beside him and take down his dictation. As soon as she came in, he looked at her, critically: 'Hm, not enough roses yet, I think,' he commented, and ordered her to take an hour-long walk in that same direction every day.

On the third day she met him on the way. He had evidently just had his bath for his hair hung in wet ringlets and his robe was slung round him hastily, leaving one shoulder bare. He always had his bath in the river, briskly pouring water over himself out of a brass vessel, while two of his disciples stood by on the steps with his towel. They were coming behind him now as he – nimbler, sprightlier than they – clambered round ledges and stones and prickly bushes. He waved enthusiastically to Daphne and called to her: 'You see, I also am enjoying fresh air and exercise!'

She waited for him to catch up with her. He was radiant: he smiled, his eyes shone, drops of water glistened on his hair and beard. 'Beautiful,' he said, and his eyes swept over the landscape, over the rocky plateau on which they stood – the holy town huddled on one side, the sky, immense and blue, melting at one edge into the mountains and at another into the river. 'Beautiful, beautiful,' he repeated and shook his head and she looked with him, and it was, everything was, the whole earth, shining and beautiful.

'Did you know we are building an ashram?' he asked her.

'Where?'

'Just here.'

He gave a short sweep of the hand, and she looked round her, puzzled. It did not seem possible for anything to grow in this spot except thistles and shrubs: and as if to prove the point, just a little way off was an abandoned site around which were scattered a few sad, forgotten bricks.

'A tip-top, up-to-date ashram,' he was saying, 'with air-conditioned meditation cells and a central dining-hall. Of course it will be costly, but in America I shall collect a good deal of funds. There are many rich American ladies who are interested in our movement.' He tilted his head upwards and softly swept back his hair with his hand, first one side and then the other, in a peculiarly vain and womanly movement.

She was embarrassed and did not wish to see him like that, so she looked away into the distance and saw the two young men who had accompanied him running off towards the ashram; they looked like two young colts, skipping and gambolling and playfully tripping each other up. Their joyful young voices, receding into the distance, were the only sounds, otherwise it was silent all round, so that one could quite clearly hear the clap of birds' wings as they flew up from the earth into the balmy, sparkling upper air.

'I have many warm invitations from America,' Swamiji said. 'From California especially. Do you know it? No? There is a Mrs. Fisher, Mrs. Gay Fisher, her husband was in shoe business. She often writes to me. She has a very spacious home which she will kindly put at our disposal and also many connections and a large acquaintance among other ladies interested in our movement. She is very anxious for my visit. Why do you make such a face?'

Daphne gave a quick, false laugh and said, 'What face?'

'Like you are making. Look at me – why do you always look away as if you are ashamed?' He put his hand under her chin and turned her face towards himself. 'Daphne,' he said, tenderly; and then, 'It is a pretty name.'

Suddenly, in her embarrassment, she was telling him the story of Daphne: all about Apollo and the laurel tree, and he seemed interested, nodding to her story, and now he was making her walk along with him, the two of them all alone and he leaning lightly on her arm. He was slightly shorter than she was.

'So,' he said, when she had finished, 'Daphne was afraid of love . . . I think you are rightly named, what do you say? Because I think – yes, I think this Daphne also is afraid of love.'

He pinched her arm, mischievously, but seeing her battle with stormy feelings, he tactfully changed the subject. Again his eyes shone, again he waved his hand around: 'Such a lovely spot for our ashram, isn't it? Here our foreign friends – from America, like yourself from U.K., Switzerland, Germany, all the countries of the world – here their troubled minds will find peace and slowly they will travel along the path of inner harmony. How beautiful it will be! How inspiring! A new world! Only one thing troubles me, Daphne, and on this question now I want advice from your cool and rational mind.'

Daphne made a modest disclaiming gesture. She felt not in the least cool or rational, on the contrary, she knew herself to have become a creature tossed by passion and wild thoughts.

But 'No modesty, please,' he said to her disclaimer. 'Who

knows that mind of yours better, you or I? Hm? Exactly. So don't be cheeky.' At which she had to smile: on top of everything else, how nice he was, how terribly, terribly nice. 'Now can I ask my question? You see, what is troubling me is, should we have a communal kitchen or should there be a little cooking place attached to each meditation cell? One moment: there are pros and cons to be considered. Listen.'

He took her arm, familiar and friendly, and they walked. Daphne listened, but there were many other thoughts rushing in and out of her head. She was very conscious of his hand holding her arm, and she kept that arm quite still. Above all, she was happy and wanted this to go on for ever, he and she walking alone in that deserted place, over shrubs and bricks, the river glistening on one side and the mountains on the other, and above them the sky where the birds with slow, outstretched wings were the only patterns on that unmarred blue.

Not only did it not go on for ever, but it had to stop quite soon. Running from the direction of the ashram, stumbling, waving, calling, came a lone, familiar figure: 'Yu-hu!' shouted Helga. 'Wait for me!'

She was out of breath when she caught up with them. Strands of blonde hair had straggled into her face, perspiration trickled down her neck into the collar of her pale cerise blouse with mother-of-pearl buttons: her blue eyes glittered like ice as they looked searchingly from Swamiji to Daphne and back. She looked large and menacing.

'Why are you walking like two love-birds?'

'Because that is what we are,' Swamiji said. One arm was still hooked into Daphne's and now he hooked the other into Helga's. 'We are talking about kitchens. Let's hear what you have to advise us.'

'Who cares for me?' said Helga, pouting. 'I'm just silly old Helga.'

'Stop thinking about yourself and listen to the problem we are faced with.'

Now there were three of them walking, and Daphne was no longer quite so happy. She didn't mind Helga's presence, but she knew that Helga minded hers. Helga's resentment wafted right across Swamiji, and once or twice she looked over his head (which she could do quite easily) to throw an angry blue glance at Daphne. Daphne looked back at her to ask, what have I done? Swamiji walked between them, talking and smiling and holding an arm of each.

That night there was an unpleasant scene. As usual, Daphne was sitting writing up her notes while Helga lay in bed and from time to time called out, 'Turn off the light' before turning round and going back to sleep again. Only tonight she didn't go back to sleep. Instead she suddenly sat bolt upright and said, 'The light is disturbing me.'

'I won't be a minute,' Daphne said, desperately writing, for she simply had to finish, otherwise tomorrow's avalanche of notes would be on top of her – Swamiji was so quick, so abundant in his dictation – and she would never be able to catch up.

'Turn it off!' Helga suddenly shouted, and Daphne left off writing and turned round to look at her. From the high thatched roof of their little room, directly over Helga's bed, dangled a long cord with a bulb at the end: it illumined Helga sitting up in bed in her lemon-yellow nylon nightie which left her large marble shoulders bare; above them loomed her head covered in curlers which made her look awesome like Medusa, while her face, flecked with pats of cream, also bore a very furious and frightening expression.

'Always making up to Swamiji,' she was saying in a loud, contemptuous way. 'All night you have to sit here and disturb me so tomorrow he will say, "You have done so much work, good girl, wonderful girl, Daphne." Pah. It is disgusting to see you flirting with him all the time.'

'I don't know what you're talking about,' Daphne said in a trembly voice.

'Don't know what you're talking about,' Helga repeated, making a horrible mimicking face and attempting to reproduce Daphne's accent but drowning it completely in her German one. 'I hate hypocrites. Of course everyone knows you English are all hypocrites, it is a well-known fact all over the world.'

'You're being terribly unfair, Helga.'

'Turn off the light! Other people want to sleep, even if you are busy being Miss Goody-goody!'

'In a minute,' Daphne said, sounding calm and continuing with her task.

Helga screamed with rage: 'Turn it off! Turn it off!' She bounced up and down in her bed with her fists balled. Daphne took no notice whatsoever but went on writing. Helga tossed herself face down into her pillow and pounded it and sobbed and raged from out of there. When Daphne had finished writing, she turned off the light and, undressing in the dark, lay down in her lumpy bed next to Helga, who by that time was asleep, still face downwards and her fists clenched and dirty tear-marks down her cheeks.

Next morning Helga was up and dressed early but contrary to her usual custom, she was very quiet and tiptoed around so as not to disturb her room-mate. When Daphne finally woke up, Helga greeted her cheerfully and asked whether she had had a good sleep, and then she told her how she had watched poor Klas stepping into a pat of fresh cow-dung on his way to meditation. Helga thought this was very funny, she laughed loudly at it and encouraged Daphne to laugh too by giving her shoulder a hearty push. Then she went off to get breakfast for the two of them, and, after they had had it, and stepped outside the room to cross over to Swamiji's, she suddenly put her arm round Daphne and whispered into her ear: 'You won't tell him anything? No? Daphnelein?' And to seal their friendship, their conspiracy, she planted a big, wet kiss on Daphne's neck and said, 'There. Now it is all well again.'

Swamiji was receiving daily letters from America, and he was very merry nowadays and there was a sense of bustle and departure about him. The current meditation course, for which Daphne and Helga and all of them had enrolled, was coming to an end, and soon they would be expected to go home again so that they might radiate their newly-acquired spiritual health from there. But when they talked among themselves, none of them seemed in any hurry to go back. The two Scottish school-teachers were planning a tour of India to see the Taj Mahal and the Ajanta caves and other such places of interest, while Klas wanted to go up to Almora, to investigate a spiritual brotherhood he had heard of there. Swamiji encouraged them – 'It is such fun to travel,' he said, and obviously he was gleefully looking forward to his own travels, receiving and answering all those airmail letters and studying airline folders, and one of the young men who attended on him had already been sent to Delhi to make preliminary arrangements.

Daphne had no plans. She didn't even think of going home; it was inconceivable to her that she could go or be anywhere where he was not. The Scottish school-teachers urged her to join them on their tour, and she half-heartedly agreed, knowing though that she would not go. Helga questioned her continuously as to what she intended to do, and when she said she didn't know, came forward with suggestions of her own. These always included both of them; Helga had somehow taken it for granted that their destinies were now inseparable. She would sit on the side of Daphne's bed and say in a sweet, soft voice, 'Shall we go to Khajurao? To Cochin? Would you like to visit Ceylon?' and at the same time she would be coaxing and stroking Daphne's pillow as if she were thereby coaxing and stroking Daphne herself.

All the time Daphne was waiting for him to speak. In London she had been so sure of what he meant her to do, without his ever having to say anything; now she had to wait for him to declare himself. Did he want her to accompany him to America; did he want her to stay behind in India; was she to go home? London, though it held her mother, her father, her job, her friends, all her memories, was dim and remote to her; she could not imagine herself returning there. But if that was what he intended her to do, then she would; propelled not by any will of her own, but by his. And this was somehow a great happiness to her: that she, who had always been so self-reliant in her judgements and actions, should now have succeeded in surrendering not only her trained, English mind but everything else as well – her will, herself, all she was – only to him.

His dictation still continued every day; evidently this was going to be a massive work, for though she had already written out hundreds of foolscap pages, the end was not yet in sight. Beyond this daily dictation, he had nothing special to say to her; she still went on her evening walk, but he did not again come to meet her. In any case, this walk of hers was now never taken alone but always in the company of Helga, whose arm firmly linked hers. Helga saw to it that they did everything together these days: ate, slept, sat with Swamiji, even meditated. She did not trust her alone for a moment, so even if Swamiji had wanted to say anything private to Daphne, Helga would always be there to listen to it.

Daphne wasn't sure whether it was deep night or very early in the morning when one of the bearded young men came to call her. Helga, innocently asleep, was breathing in and out. Daphne followed the messenger across the courtyard. Everything was sleeping in a sort of grey half-light, and the sky too was grey with some dulled, faint stars in it. Across the river a small, wakeful band of devotees was chanting and praying, they were quite a long way off and yet the sound was very clear in the surrounding silence. There was no light in Swamiji's room, nor was he in it; her guide led her through the room and out of an opposite door which led to the adjoining veranda, overlooking the river. Here Swamiji sat on a mat, eating a meal by the light of a kerosene lamp. 'Ah, Daphne,' he said, beckoning her to sit opposite him on the mat. 'There you are at last.'

The bearded youth had withdrawn. Now there were only the two of them. It was so strange. The kerosene lamp stood just next to Swamiji and threw its light over him and over his tray of food. He ate with pleasure and with great speed, his hand darting in and out of the various little bowls of rice, vegetable, lentils, and curds. He also ate very neatly, so that only the very tips of the fingers of his right hand were stained by the food and nothing dropped into his beard. It struck Daphne that this was the first time that she had seen him eat a full meal: during the course of his busy day, he seemed content to nibble at nuts and at his favourite sweetmeats, and now and again drink a tumbler of milk brought to him by one of his young men.

'Can I talk to you?' he asked her. 'You won't turn into a laurel tree?'

He pushed aside his tray and dabbled his hand in a finger-bowl and then wiped it on a towel. 'I think it would be nice,' he said, 'if you come with me to America.'

She said, 'I'd like to come.'

'Good.'

He folded the towel neatly and then pressed it flat with his hand. For a time neither of them said anything. The chanting came from across the river; the kerosene lamp cast huge shadows.

'We shall have to finish our book,' he said. 'In America we shall have plenty of leisure and comfort for this purpose . . . Mrs. Gay Fisher has made all arrangements.'

He bent down to adjust the flame of the lamp and now the light fell directly on his face. At that moment Daphne saw very clearly that he was not a good-looking man, nor was there anything noble in his features: on the contrary, they were short, blunt, and common, and his expression, as he smiled to himself in anticipation of America, had something disagreeable in it. But the next moment he had straightened up again, and now his face opposite her was full of shadows and so wise, calm, and beautiful, that she had to look away for a moment, for sheer rapture.

'We shall be staying in her home,' he said. 'It is a very large mansion with swimming-pool and all amenities – wait, I will show you.' Out of the folds of his gown he drew an envelope, which he had evidently kept ready for her and out of which he extracted some colour photographs.

'This is her mansion. It is in Greek style. See how gracious these tall pillars, so majestic. It was built in 1940 by the late Mr. Fisher.' He raised the lamp and brought it near the photograph to enable her to see better. 'And this,' he said, handing her another photograph, 'is Mrs. Gay Fisher herself.'

He looked up and saw that light had dawned, so he lowered the wick of the lamp and extinguished the flame. Thus it was by the frail light of earliest dawn that Daphne had her first sight of Mrs. Gay Fisher.

'She writes with great impatience,' he said. 'She wants us to come at once, straightaway, woof like that, on a magic carpet if possible.' He smiled, tolerant, amused: 'She is of a warm, impulsive nature.'

The picture showed a woman in her fifties in a pastel two-piece and thick ankles above dainty shoes. She wore a three-rope pearl necklace and was smiling prettily, her head a little to one side, her hands demurely clasped before her. Her hair was red.

'The climate in California is said to be very beneficial,' Swamiji said. 'And wonderful fruits are available. Not to speak of ice-cream,' he twinkled, referring to his well-known weakness. 'Please try and look a little bit happy, Daphne, or I shall think that you don't want to come with me at all.'

'I want to,' she said. 'I do.'

He collected his photographs from her and put them carefully back into the envelope. There was still chanting on the other side of the river. The river looked a misty silver now and so did the sky and the air and the mountains as slowly, minute by minute, day emerged from out of its veils. The first bird woke up and gave a chirp of pleasure and surprise that everything was still there.

'Go along now,' he said. 'Go and meditate.' He put out his hand and placed it for a moment on her head. She felt small, weak, and entirely dependent on him. 'Go, go,' he said, pretending impatience, but when she went, he called: 'Wait!' She stopped and turned back. 'Wake up that sleepy

Helga,' he said. 'I want to talk to her.' Then he added: 'She's coming with us too.' 'To America?' she said, and in such a way that he looked at her and asked, 'What's wrong?' She shook her head. 'Then be quick,' he said.

A few days later he sent her a present of a sari. It was of plain mill cloth, white with a thin red border. She put it away but when, later, he saw her in her usual skirt and blouse, he asked her where it was. She understood then that from now on that was what he wanted her to wear, as a distinguishing mark, a uniform almost, the way his bearded young attendants always wore orange robes. She put it on just before her evening walk; it took her a long time to get it on, and when she had, she felt awkward and uncomfortable. She knew she did not look right, her bosom was too flat, her hips too narrow, nor had she learned how to walk in it, and she kept stumbling. But she knew she would have to get used to it, so she persevered; it seemed a very little obstacle to overcome.

Instead of going on her usual route, she turned today in the opposite direction and walked towards the town. First she had to pass all the other ashrams, then she had to go through the little wood where the sadhus did penance, and the beggars stretched pitiful arms towards her and showed her their sores. In these surroundings, it did not seem to matter greatly, not even to herself, what she wore and how she wore it; and when she had crossed the wood, and had got to the temples and bazaars, it still did not matter, for although there were crowds of people, none of them had any time to care for Daphne. The temple bells rang and people bought garlands and incense and sweetmeats to give to their favourite gods. Daphne crossed the holy bridge and, as she did so, folded her hands in homage to the holy river. Once or twice she tripped over her sari, but she didn't mind, she just hitched it up a bit higher. When she came to the end of the bridge, she turned and walked back over it, again folding her hands and even saying, 'Jai Ganga-ji', only silently to herself and not out loud like everyone else. Then she saw Helga coming towards her, also dressed in a white sari with a red border; Helga waved to her over the heads of people and when they came together, she turned and walked back with Daphne, her arm affectionately round her shoulder. Helga was wearing her sari all wrong, it was too short for her and her feet coming out at the end were enormous. She looked ridiculous, but no one cared; Daphne didn't either. She was glad to be with Helga, and she thought probably she would be glad to be with Mrs. Gay Fisher as well. She was completely happy to be going to California, and anywhere else he might want her to accompany him.

A Young Man of Good Family

Georgia wanted to look her best, of course, but at the same time she was afraid of being late so she took her comb with her and drew it through her hair on the bus. It was there too that, peering into her compact mirror, she painted her eyes and daubed powder on her nose. She was never very good at make-up, even at the best of times, and the shaking and lurching of the ancient bus did not help. People watched her with interest, and some, like the shy little clerk next to her, with amazement; a few of them passed witty comments to each other in Hindi which of course Georgia didn't understand and that was just as well. But, in any case, she was always sublimely unself-conscious and could take stares and comments in her stride. When it was time for her to get out, she said 'Excuse me' in her ringing English voice and pushed her way out with confidence.

She ran all the way from the bus-stop to the meeting-place and got there out of breath; but she was the first. She was relieved. She hated for Ranjit to be there first, he was always so cross if he was made to wait. On the other hand, she quite enjoyed waiting, there was so much to see. They met outside the Regal cinema, a crowded but interesting spot, a popular meeting-place complicated by people going in and out of the cinema to buy tickets, others come to look at the posters and stills or just gaze around to see what went on, a shoe-shine who had had his place there between two pillars for the last fifteen years, a man selling fountain-pens, boys with the evening papers, and sated, contented people coming out of the Espresso bar next door. Georgia liked to feel herself part of the crowd, and it never occurred to her that she wasn't, that in fact her white skin and European clothes left her an island on her own in the surrounding sea of indigenous Indians. A mainly masculine sea, by the way: she was additionally odd by being feminine, and unaccompanied, unprotected, unowned feminine at that. There was no one there who didn't have a curious look and thought for her; but she was, as already stated, of an unself-conscious nature, and moreover she was at present too contented to notice anything amiss. She liked being there in that interesting crowd; she liked waiting for Ranjit; and she had the whole evening to look forward to, they would be together, he and she, and wonderful things might happen.

Ranjit's feelings, before these meetings, were considerably less pleasant. He took an even longer time than usual to knot his tie – and he was always careful about this, even when he had nowhere special to go to – and frowned at himself in the mirror as he knotted. He would have liked not to go. He thought of all the other things he could be doing instead of meeting Georgia: a game of tennis at the Club, a milkshake with friends in a restaurant to listen to the music and look at all the pretty girls; or simply to stay at home and be a credit to his parents who were entertaining this evening – a few old people like themselves, retired generals and their wives, but he would not be bored (or only in the nicest, gentlest way) because he would enjoy refilling glasses and handing round nuts and being admired for his good manners and good looks. Any of these alternatives, he thought as he knotted his tie, would be better than meeting Georgia. The nearer the time approached the more reluctant he became; he thought of how she would be standing there so conspicuously and how conspicuous he himself would become in coming to claim her. People would nudge each other and smile and say things which she could not understand but he could. The knot of his tie failed to come right and he tore it open and tore the tie from his neck and threw it on the ground and stamped his foot. After a while, however, he picked it up and started over again. Once, when similar emotions had overcome him, he had simply not gone; had stood her up. But the repercussions to that had been so severe that he knew he could not repeat the escapade, at least not until the time came when he was ready to break with her for good. Quite often he thought – as a matter of fact he was thinking it right at this moment – that the time had indeed come, but when he reflected on it more closely he found that he was not willing to do without her yet. He needed, even wanted, her for a variety of reasons which he had not analysed but which were weighty enough to prevent him from giving in to the temptation of not ever having to see her again.

This is what had happened that time when he had stood her up: instead of meeting her, he had gone to the Club with a friend; there they met some more friends, had a game or two, a drink, and then decided to order dinner. So it was late when he got home. His mother was still up and, when she heard him, she came out on the landing, combing her thin grey hair. 'Your friend was here,' she said. It seemed Georgia had made several stormy telephone calls and finally appeared at the house, in a dishevelled state and in tears. His mother told him all this calmly, even with a little smile: young people will be young people, and she knew that she could trust her Ranjit not to get involved more than was prudent. She seemed rather proud of him, if anything, and proud of herself too for being so broadminded and emancipated.

However, it was she who was woken up by the telephone in the night, and that pleased her rather less. Ranjit too was sleepy and cross.

'Listen,' said Georgia on the telephone urgently into his ear, 'I know I'm mad and your mother is furious with me, but I *had* to —'

'What's the time?' he said.

'I don't know – two o'clock or three – I couldn't sleep, I've been torturing myself to death here. Ranjit, why didn't you come? What's the matter? Have you stopped loving me?'

'Where are you speaking from?' he asked suspiciously.

'Downstairs, the landlord's. I woke them up – I was in such agony. Please tell me quickly: Ranjit? What happened? You don't want to see me again?'

'Who's listening?'

'Is it finished? Tell me, tell me. If you think I'll go on living without you —'

'Look, I'll come round first thing in the morning.'

'I don't believe you. If you hang up, I'll ring again – I'll keep ringing – all night —'

'First thing in the morning, I *swear,*' he said with all the honesty and conviction he could pack into his voice, and hung up. He was bathed in perspiration and leaned weakly against the wall; he watched the telephone and, when it rang, he picked it up and said down it, 'I swear to you by anything you want', tense and imploring.

Of course next day she was very sorry, which was just as well for now it was not he who had to apologize but she. Anyway, he forgave her and they both took the morning off, she from her job in All India Radio, he from his studies. They stayed together in her rented room, which was on the roof and very hot but cosy too, full of bits of makeshift furniture she had bought or knocked together out of old tins and packing-cases, and a lot of paperback books and artistic pictures torn out of magazines and tacked to the wall. They stayed in bed most of the time. Georgia was in a very self-critical mood, which was not uncommon, especially after she had behaved badly (which was also not uncommon). Although she made Ranjit swear to her several times that he had forgiven her, she kept coming back to the subject of her own bad behaviour the night before, and the more she dwelled on it the more monstrous she felt it to have been. The cause of her disturbance she seemed, to his relief, to have forgotten.

'I've got no self-control, that's always been my trouble,' she said, sitting up in bed and massaging her scalp to stimulate the growth of her hair. He lay back in bed, naked and sated, watching her with his arms folded behind his head. 'When I feel something,' she said and at the word 'feel' balled her fist against her heart, 'I have to get it out of my system or burst. I wish I were a lovely cool thing like you. Give me a kiss quick.' After some prodding he obliged, then sank back again on to the pillows. 'Lazy bastard,' she said, smiling affectionately, and returned to massaging her scalp. 'There's one thing I can't do, not if I live to be a hundred, and that's sit still and suffer. Well I wouldn't be here, would I, if I could?' For what had brought Georgia out to India in the first place had been her love for a young Indian whom she had met in England and then had followed out to India because she couldn't bear to wait for his letters. That affair had come to nothing, and now she swore herself black and blue that her feelings for this first boy had been nothing compared with those she had for Ranjit. Nevertheless, as she well knew, any reference to his predecessor was always an annoyance to Ranjit and, sure enough, when she turned round to look at him, there he was frowning. 'Oh goodness,' she quickly called, 'and if I hadn't come, I wouldn't have met *you*! Can you imagine it? Ranjit! Not to have met you!' She laughed at the impossibility of even imagining such a situation, but then became grave again at once, she bit her lip and looked worried: 'Was your mother very mad at me? She must have been, who wouldn't be! And this morning when I woke up and thought of what I'd done, I felt so *aw*ful, if you knew, you'd be sorry for me.' She looked at him anxiously.

'It's all right,' he said and yawned.

'It's not all right! Ranjit! Why do I do these things? Why am I such a bitch?' She closed her eyes in shame and pressed the heels of her hands hard against them. When, however, she opened them again, she was quite different, she turned to him and said: 'And don't look so innocent. Whose fault was it anyway? What happened to you? Where were you?' Now those explanations, which he had begun to hope would not be necessary, had to begin.

If at such moments the temptation to break with her for good became almost irresistible, there were others when he was pleased to have her. She was quite different from any other person he knew. Ranjit came from a good family, he had been to a good school and a good college; he prided himself on certain standards of behaviour – for instance, always being a gentleman – which everyone else he knew also tried to observe. Georgia, however, seemed to have different standards, and these made her odd and her behaviour often embarrassing. Yet at the same time there was something thrilling about her unconventional ways so that it was exciting to be with her. He was proud of her too, for his friends were always urging him to bring her to parties and restaurants, and when he did, she became the centre of attention. Their favourite restaurant was a small, very modern place, rather expensive, which had a loud band and a tiny dance-floor in it. Here they sat for many hours, smoking, drinking milkshakes, and feeling sophisticated enough to want to discuss problems of universal significance. However, although they were vaguely (even nostalgically) aware of the existence of these problems, they did not have the wherewithal to express them and so were always a little short of conversation. Their most rewarding time was when Georgia was with them, for she was articulate enough and in a way they found extremely stimulating. She was rather older than they were – nearing the end of her twenties if the truth were told which it wasn't, not by her, anyway. She liked to lean back in her chair, with her hands folded behind her head, blowing smoke-rings at the ceiling: 'Boys,' she would say, 'I've seen it all.' Yet she wasn't world-weary, even when she spoke like this; on the contrary, everything interested and excited her, starting with herself about whom she spoke more frankly than Ranjit and his friends had thought permissible. She kept nothing secret. If she had her periods and wasn't feeling too good, she would tell them loudly and clearly, so that they were hard put to it to pretend not to be embarrassed. And she was equally frank about her spiritual or mental states, which in any case it seemed to give her pleasure to dwell upon.

'I'm a bum,' she would say. 'What have I ever done? What have I achieved? Except living, of course. I've done plenty of that. Living and feeling, oh my God, yes.'

What they liked to hear best was when she told them about London and her life there. 'I had just the one black skirt, tight like *this*' – and she squeezed herself together and moulded her hands over her hips – 'and night after night I'd go dancing in this cellar. I had my hair tied up in a pony-tail so it wouldn't get in the way. We'd dance till we dropped.

'I had one friend, Jim Murphy, mad as a hatter. He'd make big placards and wear them round his neck. One week he'd go around reading "Beware the Apocalypse" and the next "Death is the Final and Most Satisfying Orgasm". One day he fell off the back of a motor-bike and bust his skull open and that was that, poor bastard.

'What about you?' she suddenly turned on them. 'I never see *you* do anything. What's wrong with you? There's the whole of India, bursting with problems, screaming for help, and all you do is sit around here drinking, God help us, milkshakes. Well, isn't anybody at least going to ask me to dance?'

One by one they went round the tiny dance-floor with her. They all of them danced very well and so did she, though in a different way. They were graceful, easy, fluid, their bodies born for dancing, whereas she made up what she lacked in natural aptitude by a lot of vigour and daring. In between she also had talk with the band, all of whom she knew by name – Sammy, Billy, Arnold – swarthy Christians from Bombay who were having trouble with the management about their fees. She shouted to them over her shoulder as she danced by and they answered her the next time round, and at midnight they had their supper at her table while Ranjit and his friends felt proud before the other clients to be thus marked out and offered cigarettes to the band and ordered ice-cream sodas for them.

Georgia often returned to the subject of what were they doing for India. She had a lot of feeling for the country and wanted every young Indian to devote himself heart and soul to its uplift. She told Ranjit all the things he ought to be doing – building dams, teaching peasants to read and write, defending the frontier – all the things *she* would be doing if only she had had the good fortune to be born an Indian. In England nowadays, she said, one felt so frustrated – there wasn't anything to do, only things to protest against. But here! a whole country to be built up! a whole nation to be revitalized! a whole culture to be awakened! 'Ranjit, how lucky you are! What opportunities!' and she dug him in the shoulder-blades as if to rouse him. He shrugged her off impatiently: such talk seemed to him just nonsense. What did she expect of him? That he should sink his caste and class, throw away all his advantages – for instance, the expensive education his parents had provided – and take up work he was not fitted for? It was all right for foreigners to talk in this strain, but people who actually lived in the country and belonged here knew that there was no place for far-fetched idealism. As far as Ranjit was concerned, the best way he could serve his country and please everyone all round was conscientiously to follow the path which had been laid down for him and on which he had already started off so well. He had acquitted himself creditably at school, had got a good second-class degree at college and had played in the University cricket team, and now he was studying hard to pass another exam and get, if possible, into the Indian Foreign Service. This was what everyone expected of him, and indeed what he expected of himself. Acquiescence came quite naturally to him, for it had never occurred to him that there could be any other goals. Now Georgia came along and said that there were. When she talked like that, she made him feel uncomfortable.

There were other things about her that made him feel uncomfortable. One of these was her friends. Her best friend was a French girl, Suzanne, who worked with her in All India Radio. She was an attractive girl with long golden hair and good legs who wore pretty dresses with frills showing underneath, and those frills, though nylon and pink, were always torn in at least one place. Suzanne had a lot of Indian boy-friends, whom she kept changing, but another friend of theirs, Jean, an English girl working in a library, had only one called Hameed who was always to be found either eating or sleeping in her room. Sometimes they all got together in the evenings and stayed till late in the night. Ranjit enjoyed these gatherings in some ways – they were so different from anything he knew – but in others they irritated him. What irritated him the most was the presence of Hameed, whom he did not like. He was a thin young man with a beard who never did any work though he claimed to be a film technician; he did not speak English well and came from goodness knows where. He was certainly not the sort of person Ranjit would have chosen for a friend, and it was therefore doubly irritating to have Hameed treating him as if there were some special bond between them. Hameed always spoke to him in Hindi, calling him friend or brother, which made Ranjit go very stiff and formal and answer back in his best English. The three girls meanwhile would be talking non-stop, and they would laugh a lot and tell each other things which Ranjit thought no person would like any other person to know; but it seemed they had no secrets from each other, nor from Hameed and Ranjit either. The atmosphere was always very relaxed, with everyone lying on the bed or on the floor or slouched in armchairs, and if it was very hot the girls thought nothing of unbuttoning their blouses or hitching their skirts high up on their thighs. They drank rather a lot of Indian whisky and, as the night wore on, they tended to become more and more lightheaded and their conversation, it seemed to Ranjit, more and more outrageous, so that he did not know where to look, especially as Hameed would be winking at him from across the room and making ribald comments in Hindi.

How different it was at one of Indira's parties! Indira was Ranjit's elder sister, who was married to a rising young oil-executive and gave very smart parties which were famous among the junior married set. She took a lot of trouble over these parties, trying out new recipes for the buffet dinner, mixing a fruit punch, turning off the lights and playing dance records by candlelight. She always liked to have Ranjit there, for she was proud of her handsome, well-mannered brother and liked to show him off. She was also glad to be able to introduce him into a wider society and so give him the opportunity of getting to know the world. She took care to invite a number of attractive unmarried girls for his benefit, for although it was of course too early to think of anything permanent, it was just as well for Ranjit to get to know the sort of girls among whom ultimately he would have to choose. That did not mean, however, that she was in the least perturbed by his liaison with Georgia: on the contrary, like her mother, she was proud of it and glad that he was getting this experience, free and gratis. Occcasionally she invited Georgia to one of her parties, but strangely enough this was never a success, for although Indira did her best to draw her out, Georgia merely sat there sullen and depressed and made no effort to join in the fun. Indira was disappointed in her, and rather surprised too, because after what Ranjit had told her (and he told her almost everything – she was not only his elder sister but also his friend and confidante) she had expected Georgia to be a great asset at these entertainments.

Ranjit was annoyed with Georgia for not being lively at Indira's parties and a credit to himself and his sister. Once they had a row about it. They had come away early from

Indira's apartment because Georgia had been so bored and unco-operative, and now Ranjit was cross and she apologetic. 'I was feeling low,' she said by way of conciliation, but that only made him more cross, he waved his hands in the air and exclaimed, 'Low, low, what does that mean? If you feel low, you stay at home in bed, you don't come and spoil other people's fun.'

'I know,' she said miserably, and after a pause, 'But I wanted to be with *you*,' and lovingly stroked his cheek.

He jerked his head away and began scowlingly to pace her room, his hands in his pockets, while she, half lying across her bed, watched him with suffering eyes. Midway he stopped pacing and stood in front of her: 'And it isn't the first time either. You're always like that when I take you to my sister's house.' He narrowed his eyes and looked at her dangerously. But how handsome he was standing there in front of her – tall, well-built, well-fed, with his thick hair and flawless skin and his large shining eyes. She pursed her lips and said sweet things to him, but he turned away impatiently and flung himself into a chair on the opposite side of the room, with his back to her and his arms crossed obstinately.

Now she too began to get angry. She got up off the bed and buttoned her blouse which had been open rather wantonly. She said, 'I can't help it, can I, if it's so damn boring at your sister's.'

He cried, 'What do you mean – boring!' and jumped up so that the chair fell over. He was genuinely shocked. He had always agreed with Indira that whatever went on at her house was the latest in chic living.

'Of course it's boring! And worse, lots worse!' said Georgia, getting angrier, though not with him now so much as with Indira and her husband and her guests: up and coming, all of them, determinedly modern, eager for a sophistication they had read about and tried hard to achieve; they called each other by witty nicknames and their conversation was freely sprinkled with yesterday's slang.

'How can people live like that – those silly parties and fancy apartments? In a country like India. It makes me sick —' and she shook herself and popped out her tongue in an expression of extreme distaste. 'Tomorrow they're having a coffee party, I heard them talking. Indira's going to take the car and drive over to some stupid bitch's house – and I can see her, you know I can't get it out of my mind, I can see her sitting in that car, ever so careful so as not to spoil her hair, and all the way she'll be thinking of that damn coffee party and who's going to be there. She won't look right or left and so of course she won't even see all those dirty hovels she has to drive past full of sick, starved people —'

'You're crazy,' Ranjit said with a contemptuous shrug. He put on his coat and stroked his hands over his hair.

'Where are you going?'

He didn't answer but went out and down the stairs. She ran after him and called down the stairs, begging him to stop. She didn't care who heard her. She didn't care either any more about India and her starving millions, although only a moment ago she had been stirred by a genuine concern; now all she wanted was that Ranjit shouldn't go away and, desperate to keep him, she was ready to say, do anything, to agree at once that Indira's way of life was much to be admired, so was Indira herself, and it was only she, Georgia, who was boring, bad-mannered, whatever he liked to call her – she was ready to concede anything if only he would stay with her.

It would not, however, be true to say that he came off

from these encounters entirely unscathed. For hours afterwards he would be uneasy and, though he tried not to, he would be thinking of what she had said. Ranjit was a good-natured boy who didn't wish any harm to anyone but wanted everyone to be as contented as he was himself. It never occurred to him that there could be any objection to the way he and his family lived: as he saw it, this was the station in life to which they had been born and in which it was their natural right and duty to remain. There were people poorer than they were, naturally, just as there were people richer. He knew that there was a terrible problem of poverty in India, but he did not see what he himself could do about it. It just seemed a law of nature one could not protest against. He and his family were never unkind to the poor, they had every sympathy for them and treated their servants very well and provided them with warm clothes in the winter and medicines when they were sick and gave sweets to their children at Diwali time. What more could they, could anyone do? Yet there was Georgia expecting them to do more and giving him a bad conscience about something that was not in the least his fault. He thought of her friend Jim Murphy who wore placards round his neck. Ranjit could never do a thing like that and he wouldn't want to either. It was just making a fool of oneself, and for nothing, just for a gesture. Ranjit wasn't interested in making gestures; all he wanted was to be, like his father, a good and useful member of society. Why should she keep talking to him about someone like Jim Murphy and, for some mysterious reason, succeed in making him feel guilty every time she did so? It wasn't as if Jim Murphy had ever done anything wonderful or even useful; *and* he was dead now.

Once Ranjit and Georgia went to a film. It was an American comedy about a New York professional woman in spectacles and a bun who became a glamorous blonde when she fell in love. Ranjit liked it very much and laughed as loudly as everyone else at the jokes and comical situations. So he was surprised and annoyed to hear Georgia suddenly groaning next to him, 'For God's sake let's get out, I can't stand another minute of this.' He stopped laughing for a moment, gave her a sideways look, and then continued laughing. After a while she said, 'If you're not coming, I'll go alone.' He didn't answer and didn't take his eyes off the screen. She waited a while longer and then left, rather brutally pushing her way out and disturbing the whole row. He saw the film to the end and, though he continued laughing, most of his pleasure was spoiled.

Afterwards he found her leaning against his father's car which he had borrowed for the evening. He frowned and took no notice of her but unlocked the door and slid into the driver's seat. She rapped loudly on the glass of the opposite door. He would have liked to drive away without letting her in, but when he thought of the uninhibited fuss she would undoubtedly make, he decided otherwise and leaned over to unlock the door for her. She was inside in no time, sinking into the seat and blowing her cheeks out in a *whoof* of relief. 'I thought you'd never be coming,' she reproached him. 'I've been standing here having the most indecent proposals made to me.' He blushed slightly and concentrated on getting his car out of its parking space. This was not easy for the road was cluttered with other cars starting, and the crowds who had come out of the cinema, and the rickshaw-drivers and food-sellers plying for their custom.

'How you can sit through that offensive slush,' she accused him some more.

He compressed his lips and said, 'I liked it.'

Her reply to this was lost, for just then a vast hooting of cars rose up, each one demanding space from the others. Ranjit too pressed his horn and kept it pressed. A beggar-woman appeared at his window and opened her mouth wide and pointed into it to show how hungry she was; then she rubbed her stomach. When Ranjit took no notice, she thrust her hand, a dirty claw, through the window and touched him. He shrank away and had already opened his mouth to start cursing her when suddenly he recollected himself and, with a tiny, guilty look sideways at Georgia, he dug his hand into his pocket and brought out some coins which he gave to the beggar; she mumbled her lips as she counted them and moved off without thanks.

At last their car untangled itself from the others, and they sped clear from the cinema. Georgia was looking at Ranjit with a cynical smile. She said, 'I suppose you feel lovely and good?'

As a matter of fact, he did; he always had a little glow of virtuous feeling whenever he gave money to a beggar.

'Little Master Bountiful,' said Georgia and smiled some more so that he became angry and confused. What did she want of him? There was nothing wrong, surely, in an act of charity such as he had just performed – on the contrary, it was what she always demanded of him and it had been partly for her sake, to impress and please her, that he had done it. But it seemed it had not been the right thing; just as his liking the film had not been right, although it was a good film and everyone else had enjoyed it too. Bewildered, humiliated, not knowing what to think, not wanting to talk to her, he stared straight ahead at the road and accelerated the car. This she liked; she hugged herself with both arms and laid back her head and let the wind sweep her hair. 'Faster!' she urged him, and though he too was in a daredevil mood, he looked at the speedometer and slowed down a bit for it was his father's car and he had to be careful.

It was in this way she changed him: by making scenes in which he became unsure of himself and didn't know what was expected of him. Yet he was, by nature and right of birth, a supremely confident young man; even physically, as could be seen by the way he carried himself and wore his clothes and moved every inch the most popular boy in the class. Confidence was part of his constitution, and the lack of it, for him, almost a sickness. His mother and sister were quick to notice his disturbance and equally quick to locate its cause. It was their habit to meet several times a week and thoroughly discuss all matters of interest relating to the family. Although they conducted their social life mainly in high-class educated Indian English, when they were alone together and talking family business, they invariably did so in very fast, intimate, cosy Punjabi, each with her feet up and playing with her toes. They were much alike and were proud of each other, the daughter proud of the mother for having kept up the family traditions with such gloss and polish, the mother of the daughter for having taken them over from her and maintaining them with the same care. They were not intelligent women, but they had sure instincts for what was to the family's advantage and knew how to manage things and manipulate them to their own ends. This was a legacy left to them by all their grandmothers who had had no weapons to hand – no education, no opportunities ever to leave their kitchens – other than intuition and cunning.

Georgia was just the opposite: she didn't know how to manage anything. One day she found herself dispossessed of her flat, and when Ranjit came to see her, he saw her helplessly standing in the middle of a heap of rubbish which was her furniture now dismantled and revealed for what it was – old packing-cases and empty tins of cooking fat.

'I've got to clear out in three days,' she said mournfully.

'Where will you go?'

'If only I knew.'

He was silent. He was afraid she would ask to be put up in his father's house. How impossible that would be; unthinkable. He looked again at her shabby, almost disreputable possessions, and thought of them standing around on his mother's carpets. He shuddered.

'Suzanne is having landlord trouble too, otherwise I could've dumped myself on her. And Jean has only the one room, and of course Hameed's in there with her most of the time – I'd hardly be very welcome there, would I?' She giggled slightly and looked at him to share the joke. But he was too upset and could only stand there, biting his lip and worrying. Suddenly she burst out laughing: 'Oh, come on,' she said, 'what's it matter.' She gave him a hug and a quick kiss on the cheek. 'Let's have a drink,' she said, and before long she had them both sitting quite comfortably on what was left of the furniture with a bottle of rum between them, and although he knew the situation was serious and should be considered seriously, he could not help, under her influence and that of the rum, becoming as lighthearted as she seemed to be.

Indira got ready for a really serious talk with Ranjit. She settled herself on her sofa, pulled her sari round her shoulders, and said, 'Now then.' She had shut the door and given the servants instructions not to be disturbed; she wanted a good long talk – 'Just the two of us' she told Ranjit with a smile, and he too smiled for he enjoyed long talks with his sister. Today she began by speaking about his studies, and because he knew he had been neglecting them, he answered her with exaggerated seriousness and then tried to get on to something else. He and Indira usually discussed far more interesting subjects than his studies. But today, to his surprise and slight annoyance, she kept coming back to how important it was for him to concentrate on his work and to pass if possible into the Foreign Service. He felt uncomfortable, for he already had a notion that he would not pass this exam, which would of course be disappointing but not in any way disastrous, for his father sat on enough boards and had enough influence to find a berth for him elsewhere; and meanwhile there was really no point in getting oneself upset by thinking too much of what was yet to come. So he tried to turn the conversation, tried to confide in her as usual about Georgia; but, unlike on other such occasions, Indira showed no interest in the subject, she only smiled rather coldly, and looked into the distance, and delicately scratched her head with her long, pink-painted fingernail; so that he fell silent, and then she sighed and said, 'Yes, Ranjit, nowadays study, study, study, that is how your days must be spent.'

By the time Ranjit left his sister, she had, without mentioning Georgia again, made it quite clear to him that it was time this affair came to an end. After thinking it over, he decided that Indira was right: his association with Georgia was not doing him any good at all. He began to have angry thoughts against her, and all her shortcomings bristled up in his mind. He saw her sitting in the middle of her old tins and packing-cases, laughing and drinking rum, he saw her with her friends Suzanne and Jean, all three of them untidy, sluttish, talking sex. He disliked her. She was a dispossessed tenant, a disreputable person, and as such had no right to enter into his life. For a few days he stayed at home and did nothing but sit in his room and study. He was aware of and consciously enjoyed, as he had never done before, the calm atmosphere in his house, the scrupulous regularity of meal-times, the solid furniture, the richly-hung, well-lined curtains, the silver, the table-linen; he breathed in the air of his home with relish, knowing that it was the right stuff for the lungs he had been born with. In the evenings he played whist with his parents. When Georgia rang, as she did several times, he told the servant to say he was out.

On Wednesday Indira came for lunch; she always did this on Wednesdays, unless she had a bridge-party on. After lunch they sat in the drawing-room and Indira and the mother had one of their talks while Ranjit lay on the sofa and leafed through a magazine. He had eaten rather too much, and felt heavy and sleepy, so could not concentrate very well either on his magazine or the conversation. Indira was doing most of the talking, he noticed, and her voice came to him in a pleasant, familiar drone.

'There was one in a sort of blue – no, blue-green – Conjeevaram, lovely, Rs. 185. Yes, it's a lot but what to do? I fell in love with it, on the spot, that's all.' She gave a gay laugh, popped a handful of raisins into her mouth, then stretched herself luxuriantly; it was cool in the room, the air-conditioner was on. 'Oh, Mummy,' she said, 'yesterday I had such an annoying day, what shall I tell you. It was that Babu Lal again – what we have to put up with from our servants, dear oh dear. And yesterday of all days, when the Maliks had at last kindly consented to have drinks with us – I'm just joking, they're the sweetest couple but of course terribly in demand, Anita is the prettiest thing and Bunny so witty and a very very rising young man, that you can take from me. I wish you'd have come, Ranjit. I don't know why you didn't. Bunny Malik is exactly the sort of person you ought to be meeting. Ranjit? Are you asleep?'

Ranjit wasn't really asleep but almost. In any case he was too sleepy to answer, and even if he hadn't been, he could hardly have told Indira that he was glad he hadn't met Bunny Malik and that he had no desire to do so.

'What haven't I done for that Babu Lal – clothes,' said Indira, beginning to tick off her fingers, 'my own doctor when he's sick, a nice dry quarter for him and his family.'

'He's very comfortable with you,' said her mother.

'All right, one doesn't ask for gratitude, but at least – I beg you – a little human decency and consideration!'

'Don't upset yourself, child. They are all the same, these people. Whatever you do for them.'

Ranjit went to sleep around this point, but when he woke up again, he found he remembered a lot of what he had heard. It weighed on him, although there had been nothing unusual in it, nothing that he hadn't heard plenty of times before, all his life long. He knew his mother and sister were not unkind, and moreover, he loved them and did not wish to condemn them. But the way they had spoken depressed him and made him want to get away from them, and from the house, to somewhere quite different.

Next day he overheard his mother speaking on the telephone. She spoke in a hushed voice and gave nervous looks upwards at the staircase to make sure he wasn't coming down it. As it happened, however, he *was* coming down it and he heard her saying, 'He is too busy with his studies, he must not be disturbed', but when she saw him, she lowered her voice still further and then quickly replaced the receiver. They faced each other at the bottom of the stairs but she looked beyond him and tapped the side of her nose with a preoccupied air as if she were full of thoughts which had nothing whatsoever to do with him. He knew, however, that they had everything to do with him and that she had just been talking to Georgia. He was annoyed; he hadn't particularly wanted to talk to Georgia on the telephone, but now he felt resentful at being prevented without being asked. That day he didn't do any studying but walked around the house and garden with his hands in his pockets and kicking an imaginary football before him. When his mother spoke to him, he answered her in gruff monosyllables and then pretended not to notice the anxious looks she threw after him. In the evening he refused to play whist with his parents and went out to meet his friends in their favourite restaurant.

They were glad to see him, but disappointed that he hadn't brought Georgia. And after a while he had to admit to himself that it *was* boring without her. He and his friends did not have all that much to say to one another, and they missed the sense of excitement, the breath of other worlds, which she so effortlessly infused into the air around her. Now that she was not there, everything seemed dull, even the restaurant which they had once thought so gay. A few couples were shuffling round the dance-floor, clumsy, dowdy, slow, holding each other gingerly and staring over each other's shoulders into the distance with solemn faces. And the band too seemed today slow and bored, and indeed looked rather worried as if they were suffering from indigestion or money troubles. Ranjit greeted them cordially but all he got in return were brief nods; and when it was time for their supper, they sat far away in a corner and ate in silence with their heads lowered. Ranjit got up to talk to them; he tried to be friendly and easy the way Georgia was with them, asking about their troubles with the manager and their next booking, but he could hear for himself that he didn't sound in the least like Georgia. Strangely enough, the person he did sound like was his father – he could hear it for himself, to his annoyance and shame, the way his voice went heavy and patronizing like his father's did when he tried to talk in a friendly, hearty manner to people not of his own class. They did not ask him to sit down, and when they had finished eating, they pulled out packets of cheap cigarettes and lit them and sullenly blew smoke-rings out of their mouths. Ranjit longed to offer them his own better brand of cigarettes but he did not dare to do so. He returned to his table, feeling dissatisfied and vaguely ashamed, and soon left the restaurant. Outside, though it was late by now, about eleven o'clock, the usual very small boys were still trying to sell the evening papers; they made brave attempts to keep up their usual sales patter, but they looked listless and their eyes were dim with sleepiness. Ranjit noticed that their feet were bare and their clothes ragged, and one little boy's shirt was torn all the way down the back leaving a frail pair of shoulder-blades exposed – and of course Ranjit knew this had to be so, it was always so; nevertheless he felt his heart to be heavy at the sight, and he wished things could be otherwise.

He went straight to Jean's room. She told him that Georgia had been staying with Suzanne, but now Suzanne too had been thrown out of her flat and so both of them were sharing a room in a hotel at the back of the station. She wrote down the address for him, and while she was doing this, Hameed, who was sprawled across the bed and cracking walnuts for himself, invitingly extended his palm with some peeled pieces of walnut on it. Ranjit stiffly refused and left as quickly as possible. He was tempted for a moment to go home. He did not relish the idea of going at this time of night to seek an unknown hotel at the back of the station and find there two rootless girls incongruously squatting in some squalid little room. On the other hand, he was equally reluctant to go back to his own home where he belonged. For the first time in his life it seemed to him that he did not belong there. He felt bewildered and slightly afraid. He began to walk aimlessly through the streets where he found himself, city streets with shuttered shops and sleeping figures huddled here and there in doorways. At a corner a man accosted him and offered to take him to a nice place to hear a little singing; he came very close to Ranjit and smiled into his face, showing tiny white teeth and his gums red in his betel-stained mouth. He smelled very strongly of rose perfume. Ranjit briefly shook his head and walked faster, thrusting his hands deep into his pockets as if for protection; he had been accosted by pimps often enough before, but only when he had been with a lot of friends and they could afford to laugh and be bold, manly, and rude in their reply. He came to a main thoroughfare, and here there was a little traffic and a cruising taxi slowed down for him. He got in and sank with relief against the dirty upholstery. All the windows were shut, and the car was filled with a dense, unpleasant smell. For a moment it seemed to Ranjit that this smell was one of rose perfume, but then realized that it was only of sweat and ill-washed bodies. Probably the taxi-driver and his cleaner or some other friend slept in it at nights.

The entrance to Georgia's hotel was up a staircase between a grain merchant and a radio repair shop. Everyone was asleep, and it took Ranjit a quarter of an hour before he found someone to lead him to the right room. As it happened, it was the only room in the hotel with the light still on. Suzanne, in brief black underwear, sat brushing her hair, and Georgia lay on the bed smoking. The room had no furniture except for two rather large string-beds and some shelves let into the whitewashed walls; a naked bulb dangled from the ceiling which showed a lot of cracks. But all round the room, hung like festive lanterns or balloons from odd nails drooping out of the wall, were Suzanne's dresses and frilly petticoats; a row of high-heeled, pastel-coloured shoes were ranged against one wall. There was a smell of perfume, cigarettes, and insect powder. Suzanne, her hairbrush resting for a moment against her golden hair which lay bunched thickly over one shoulder, turned towards the door and said 'Look who's here' in her teasing French accent; the fact that he had caught her in a state of advanced undress didn't seem to bother her in the least.

Georgia sat up on the bed; she stared at Ranjit and exhaled a lot of cigarette smoke and with it she said '*Well*', like an additional volley of smoke.

'Jean told me where you were.'

'I thought you'd given me up.' She tried to sound light, but at the same time she stubbed out her cigarette on the floor, pressing it down with the heel of her slipper, and there was nothing light about the way she did that. Suzanne, watching her, smiled and said, 'Don't get excited, he is not worth it.' The very next moment and as if this had been a signal, Georgia did get excited.

'I've been ringing and ringing, but always young master was out. And then your mother said you were not to be disturbed —'

'It's my exams,' he put in quickly.

'He work very hard,' said smiling Suzanne.

'What is this? Why don't you speak out? If you want to get rid of me, okay, but at least say so, don't leave it to your mother!' Her arms hung down by her sides, and she looked helpless, hurt, and angry.

Ranjit didn't know what to reply. He still stood by the door. He didn't dare look at Georgia, neither at Suzanne whose nakedness was like some pillar of fire which would burn him up if he as much as glanced in that direction. Yet the room was so small, and he so close to, hemmed in with, both of them.

'Are you coming in or going out?' Georgia said irritably. 'Because if you're coming in, then *come* in, don't stand there clinging to the door —'

He took a couple of steps forward and this brought him even closer to Georgia. There was a moment's pause during which her face grew red. Then suddenly she threw herself against his chest and clung to him. 'I've missed you, *missed* you,' she said from between clenched teeth. He glanced over her head towards Suzanne who was minding her own business, getting ready for bed.

Georgia drew back and wiped her eyes and sat down on the edge of the bed. 'I kept thinking – what if I don't see him again.' She patted the place next to her and he sat there and she held him again and hugged him close. 'Now I'll never let you go, never never.' She put her hand under his chin and turned his face towards her own and then tried to make him smile by smiling at him herself. 'Don't be afraid,' she said. 'I don't mean that. As a matter of fact, I'm going away. Look at Suzanne. She's laughing at us.'

'Good night,' said Suzanne emphatically, and lay down on her bed with her back to them.

'Can't we go somewhere else?' said Ranjit, looking at this back which was really very attractive.

'It's all right . . . Listen, Ranjit, Suzanne and I are going to Ceylon. She's got a friend there who's bought an island. It's supposed to be fantastic this island, huge orchids and a lot of fish.'

'How long for?'

'I don't know. Till we get fed up. From there we may go

on somewhere else – what do you think of Japan? We might get jobs there, or push on to California. We've been talking a lot these last few days. It's Suzanne's idea really. She says, what are we hanging around here for? She's had a lot of disappointments too . . . Don't look like that. As if you cared. If you did, if I thought you'd say just once – you think I'd go? You think wild horses could drag me from this place? Just one *whisper* from you.'

He didn't say anything, and after a moment of this silence, she laughed. She drew him down to lie beside her on the bed and began to kiss him. He was roused but struggled against himself and against her and got up. He smoothed his hair, pulled down his bush-shirt, breathed hard. 'I'm going,' he said. 'I'm not used to, with someone else in the room.' He wanted to hit Georgia. How he hated to be here, in this hotel room, trapped between these two women and the frilly dresses and feminine smells. He felt outraged and knew what he ought to do was leave at once and never come back again. But there was something else too, which added to his fury and at the same time coloured it with sorrow, and that was the idea that she who had made him what he now was – or rather, who had begun to unmake him from what he had been – should be threatening to go away and leave him to – what? His parents, Indira, his career, his future.

He had already half opened the door, but he shut it again and came striding back to the bed and towered over her: 'What do you mean – Japan?'

She sat up on the bed and began to take pins out of her hair.

'You can't go now,' he said.

'Then what? Wait around here for when you're not busy with your *exams*?'

'You can't leave me here – like this —'

'Like what? What've you got to complain about?'

'I don't want you to go,' he said weakly. For a moment he was almost tempted to say more, to offer her inducements to stay, but restrained himself in time.

2

THE SUFFERERS

An Indian Citizen

Neat in his person and just as neat the room he left behind him, Dr. Ernst fastened the padlock on his door and dropped the key into his top pocket. The padlock – supplied by the authorities – was huge, and if someone happened to be passing while he was locking up, he often pretended that he had got his finger caught in it. 'Oooh,' he would say and wave his hand painfully in the air and purse his mouth for a soundless whistle. But it was not a joke he ever made in the mornings. In the mornings, he knew, everyone was far too busy to take any notice of him, let alone of his jokes.

The apartment block in which he had been fortunate enough to get a room was one occupied mainly by assistant editors in the Publications Division or section officers in the Ministry of Education – all of them civil servants in the medium income groups, whose energies in the morning were concentrated on reaching the office in time. Since bicycles were beneath their dignity and none of them was rich enough to possess a car, getting to the office meant getting on to a bus, and it was this task ahead that accounted for the grim, determined expression on their faces. The ladies strode along purposefully in their saris, all of them intellectual ladies, graduates, wage-earners, emancipated and on an equal footing with men – the pride of modern India! Some of them grasped short umbrellas with an air which made it clear that, if necessity demanded, they would be using them to sharp effect later in the bus queue.

Dr. Ernst had no office to go to, but all the same he got up and went out at the same time as everyone else in the mornings. He felt better that way, not left out of anything but part of a busy world. Once, for a short glorious time, he too had been an office worker. He had helped to put out bulletins in the Ministry of Information and compile a weekly news-sheet on the eradication of household pests. He had been very happy, though of course he had not expected to be kept long; he had known that, sooner or later, the job would have to be handed over to a genuine Indian subject (and not an 'ersatz' one, as he liked in fun to call himself). But it had been good while it lasted – not only the working in an office on regular hours like everyone else, but also the knowledge that on the first week of every month a sufficient salary would infallibly turn up.

He walked among the crowd of office-goers towards the main gate, here and there raising his panama hat – worn as much for decorum and decoration as to shield him against the sun – in a greeting that was courtly but at the same time unobtrusive, so that those who were in too much of a hurry could, with a good conscience, pretend they hadn't noticed. One or two of the hurrying figures he looked after with pleasure: Miss Jaya, from Room No. 146–A, a valued employee in the Ministry of Culture and Scientific Affairs, walking slim and neat and upright in a green patterned sari and her hair balanced on her head in a shining coil. Youth, thought Dr. Ernst with a smile, youth and energy and confidence – the future! – and he smiled again and thrust out his chest, looking after pretty Miss Jaya, and felt as if he had been fired with an ideal, a confirmation that life was, or could be, beautiful and good.

'Ernst!'

It was Lily. She was looking out of the window of her room with a dismal air. All the windows in the block were crossed with iron bars to keep the burglars out, and Lily peering through the bars, her head to one side, her hair drooping sadly over her eyes, reminded him of a symbolical painting he had once seen and been much moved by entitled 'Humanity'. However, he was not moved by Lily; he had seen her too often, looking just like this.

'Come in and see me,' said Lily in a voice as dismal as her face.

Suppressing a sigh, lingering with a last fond look on the disappearing figure of brisk Miss Jaya, he turned aside and entered Lily's room.

'Right in,' she commanded, as he stood hesitating within the door.

He never liked to go into Lily's room. It was strange how different it was from his own, even though the rooms were absolutely standard both in construction and in their basic furnishings. These latter were supplied by the authorities and consisted of a file cupboard for a wardrobe, a serviceable wooden bed, and a dressing-table which was really only an office desk with a mirror attached. Lily had a vivid taste, and she had smothered those bare necessities in curtains, cushions, rugs, hangings, masks, prints – all oriental, all folk-art, and all very dirty. Dr. Ernst, on the other hand, had added almost nothing to the room he had been given; he really didn't have anything, except two wooden bears from Switzerland which were meant to serve as bookends, a photograph of his parents in an oval frame, and a thirty-year-old alarm clock which still kept excellent time. But he was scrupulous about maintaining everything absolutely neat and clean and scrubbed. He did this himself every morning, with a bucket and soap-suds and a brush and a lot of vigour, his sleeve rolled up over his thin arm; in summer, when there were dust-storms and everything in the city was covered in thick layers of dust, and one could even taste it gritty between one's teeth, he would carefully wipe his yellow duster over everything in his room as many as four, five, six times a day. Anything out of place, any disorder or grime anywhere in his own room, was to him like a giving in to that chaos which seemed perpetually to lie in wait for him and had done so ever since he had started on his enforced travels, almost thirty years ago.

'I feel so awful,' Lily wailed. She was squatting under the window on a little couch she had made out of old boxes covered with a thick hand-spun cloth featuring block-printed horses and riders. 'There's something terribly wrong with me.'

Dr. Ernst managed to look sympathetic, though secretly he thought that all that was wrong with Lily was the lack of a good scrub and bath. How trim Miss Jaya had looked, how neat and smart and ready for her work! Lily sagged on her couch in a crumpled flowered wrap, her face too white and a bit puffy, and her hair a tangled, clotted nest.

'No office today?' asked Dr. Ernst.

She looked at him as if he had done her an injury: 'In my state,' she said in a robust enough voice.

In his heart he condemned her. She never appreciated how lucky she was to have a job here, even though she was English. She worked as a monitor in All India Radio – in the Chinese section, strangely enough – and instead of being grateful, she carried on as if she were being exploited, frequently skipped days, and grumbled about her salary.

'I want you to phone Chinky-Linky for me,' she was saying. 'Tell him I won't be in today, so he'll have to do some *work* for once in his life. That'll be a nice change for him. I'd always been given to understand that the Chinese were an industrious race, but judging by Chinky-Linky – Oh do sit down,' she said. 'You're making me nervous.'

Dr. Ernst fidgeted: 'I have to get going.'

'What for? You're no wage-slave like the rest of us. You lucky sod. Go *on*,' she said, pointing an impatient foot at a disintegrating cane hassock on which he then had gingerly to lower himself.

He sat, uncomfortable and ill at ease, his thin knees pressed together, while she talked. As always, she had plenty to say. She had a rather whining sort of voice, which rose and fell; it was loud while she was in the middle of her subject, then sank into a mumble as her interest in it diminished, and rose again as she started on something new. In between, her servant – a crafty old man in a pair of tattered striped pyjama-trousers, who did rather well out of her by means of little commissions he paid himself out of the bazaar money – served them with cups of coffee. Dr. Ernst, always ready for refreshments, would have drunk his with pleasure, if he had not noticed a smudge of lipstick on the rim. He put the cup aside; he was still, in spite of his hardships, fastidious in these matters.

And now Lily had got on to her best subject of all and the one which always formed the climax of her conversations: her latest love affair. She had been in India for some three years now, and in that space of time had already been in love several times. Hers was a passionate nature, and indeed it was passion that had got her out to India in the first place: in pursuit of a handsome young Indian, who may have made her certain promises in London but did not feel up to them once he had safely reached home ground. She had hardly got over that disappointment, when she was in love again; and from there she never looked back, passing from passion to passion, each one more burning and more hopeless than the last.

'He was so beastly to me,' she was complaining. 'Wouldn't speak to me properly, made me pay for the dinner – he's such a brute.' But when she said 'brute', her eyes lit up and she leaned forward – smiling, eager – to say, 'So handsome! Isn't he the handsomest, handsomest creature you've ever seen?' and she pushed Dr. Ernst's knee quite hard in her anxiety for his assent and affirmation.

He couldn't quite remember this latest young man and may have confused him with one or two of his predecessors. But he said, 'Terribly, terribly handsome', and smiled at her with his perfect, pearly plate of teeth. At that moment he forgave her the smudge of lipstick on the coffee-cup and much else besides. He admired her perseverance, her refusal to compromise: all her young men had been excessively handsome and desirable, and not one of them had even remotely returned her feelings. They made her suffer, and yet she chose only them, only these paragons, and never stooped to measure her affections to a lesser man more within her range. Only the best was good enough for her, and she would go on desiring it, though doomed for ever to consume herself in her own flame.

'You should see him with his clothes off,' she indelicately told him. 'Like a god. *Such* shoulders, so broad, and hips, you don't know how slender, like a boy's. Even to think of it – oh I can't bear it!' She moaned with joy and hugged herself tight and her wrap fell apart revealing her legs, which were pale and plump, with the flesh shaking like a dewlap from the underside of the thighs.

How old was she now? Thirty? Thirty-two? Still young by his standards, but he knew that she would never marry; just as he never had. For he too had been like her, had loved and desired only what was infinitely beyond him. He had wanted to marry and had had visions of the bliss that would be waiting for him in that state; but his one condition had always been that his partner should be a paragon, and he would settle for nothing less. This trend of his had started long ago at school, where he had loved little Lise Fruhlingsfeld, pert in frilly apron and kid boots, who never looked at him without a scornful toss of her blonde mane (topped by a blue satin ribbon); while little Sophie Mann, who truly loved him and was ever eager to share her ham roll with him in the lunch break, could not get as much as a look or a thought from him. Yes, he could have married many times over – later in Amsterdam, in Beirut, in Bombay – but it was always to the Sophie Manns for whom he had no time to spare because he was too busy being in love with the Lise Fruhlingsfelds. So here he was now, sixty and single, though not sorry for it because he had kept his ideal uncompromised and still, however improbably, within his reach.

Lily crooned softly: 'I think he's got a terribly cruel streak in his nature.' Then she added: 'They all have. All these Indian men . . . I think they like to humiliate us.' She sounded very easy and even rather pleased about it, as if she liked being humiliated.

'No psycho-analysis please,' said Dr. Ernst. 'I hear it's out of fashion.'

'And you know they always pretend to like our white skins and admire us, but really I think – yes, I'm sure, I'm sure, they *despise* us.'

'What are you saying!' cried Dr. Ernst.

'Hate and despise us,' she said with relish.

He got up in indignation; he would not hear such things spoken. Indians had always been so kind to him, and he owed them so much: a place to live, a nationality, friendship, respect – all this they had given him. He said, very primly and in rebuke: 'Most of my friends are Indians.'

Lily made a rude sound. 'Like hell they are. You hardly know any, for all you've been here donkeys' years.' And when she saw him about to protest, she cried, 'All right, name them, name them!'

Without hesitation, and proudly, he stood and ticked off his fingers: 'Sri Manohar, Minister of Moral Reformation; Her Highness of Palangkot; Dr. Lall, M.P. —'

'You call those friends? Why, you're just their' – she shrugged and said in her careless, rude, English way – 'their hanger-on.'

Dr. Ernst was, as he had every right to be, insulted. He compressed his lips and his face took on a vicious expression. He had always been a mild and friendly person, but if he felt himself insulted by people whom he did not consider his superiors, he wanted to take some kind of revenge. When he had been a student of philology at the university, there had been a group of students – crude, unmannerly fellows – who had not been very nice to him, so that when he had caught one of them cheating in the examinations, he had not hesitated to report him to the authorities. This had ultimately led to the young man's expulsion, but Dr. Ernst had not been sorry: quite on the contrary, the memory of this act filled him even today with a sense of righteousness and justice done.

He told Lily in a trembling voice, 'You can go and phone your Chinky-Linky yourself.' He looked at her and felt prompted to home-truths: 'There is nothing wrong with you that you can't go to your office, only you need to wash, that is all, and tidy up this room which is not fit for a human being to live in.'

She wasn't the least bit offended, but laughed in a genuine, frank way: 'A veritable pig-sty, don't I know it. Oh, don't be cross. Sit down, I want to talk.'

But he was offended, and as a mark of disrespect put on his panama hat right there in the room and walked out of the door, ignoring the plaintive shouts she let out after him through the iron bars.

He was still upset when he reached the road, but once he started walking, his mood changed. How lucky we are, he thought, always a blue sky – and he looked at it, with an almost proprietary smile, and it really was an undeniable unflecked irreproachable blue, and the sun shining not too hot yet, and the air high and clear. The morning office rush was over, and only a few slim young college girls in freshly laundered saris stood at the bus-stop. The streets here were broad and unpaved and lined thickly with very tall, very stately trees in different shades of green. Set back far from the road, each one in its own beautifully kept garden, were white houses with pillars and verandas; their gates were ornamental and at some of them hovered little groups of servants (the bearer, the gardener, the watchman). An elderly lady went slow and stately under her parasol, and a servant in white uniform was walking a beautifully groomed Alsatian on a leather lead. Everything was leisured and green that morning, with many kinds of birds singing and twittering from out of the trees. Under such conditions, who would brood over personal feelings, over a slight received? Certainly not Dr. Ernst; he had passed too long a life, and one too full of setbacks, not to be able to shake off passing moods and take full advantage of whatever moments of happiness were offered to him. He breathed the fragrant air, listened to the birds and looked at the college girls. And who was Lily, anyway? He hummed to himself, some gay tune which rose from goodness knows what depths of past contentment to his lips.

But he had not yet decided where to go. Other people went out to work every morning, he went out to put himself in the way of work. Keeping up his contacts, he called it;

and certainly, one had to make people realize that one was still there and still ready to oblige: so that when someone heard of someone who wanted German lessons or French lessons or Latin (he was willing to teach anything, even Viennese, he often joked), then the first person they would think of, if they had recently seen him, would be Dr. Ernst. Especially as he was always so grateful: he would thank people effusively, over and over, in his most gallant, continental way, so that they felt pleased and began to have as high an opinion of themselves as he obviously did; and to repeat this pleasant sensation, they often went out of their way to recommend him elsewhere as well.

He walked along the road and thought about whom to visit this morning. He felt inclined not only to keep up contacts but also to spend a pleasant morning chatting with friends. The nicest place to go was, of course, Maiska's, and already his thoughts and footsteps were turned in that direction. It was always cosy at Maiska's. She was a middle-aged European woman, plain, dowdy, yet with a charm born of good-nature and sympathy which made her the centre of a whole group of friends. No one ever called her by her first name, whatever that may have been, or by her married name which was a Bengali one for at one stage she had had a Bengali husband: but always simply by her maiden surname, Maiska. She had a job in the University, teaching various European languages – she knew a great number of them, and it was said she had even learned Bengali during her brief married life – and she lived in a flat near the University, in an area which was rather shabby and crowded, in a house equally shabby and crowded, with dirty stairs and choked drains. But once inside Maiska's flat, everything was quite different. Although she had in her furnishings largely made use of cheap Indian handloom materials, somehow the total effect was completely, cosily European. There were many ashtrays, usually well filled with stubs, and comfortable armchairs to sit in, and good pictures on the walls, and good books in the bookcases.

Dr. Ernst had spent some of his best hours there. Maiska really knew how to make one feel at home, and there were usually one or two other friends with her, members of that band of displaced lonely Europeans, like Lily and Dr. Ernst himself, who constantly gravitated round her flat. Only the week before they had had a lovely party there, the Linskys had brought potato salad, and Anna Shukla had baked one of her cheese-cakes, and Herman had showed them a whole range of new card-tricks (he was so clever, they had all agreed, a real magician). Evenings at Maiska's were the best, but even during the day it was a very pleasant place to visit. He was already looking forward to the cup of coffee she would serve him – good, strong, European coffee not like Lily's weak English brew which always tasted as if it had come out of a bottle – and wondering, and rather hoping, if he would meet any other of their friends there: Anna Shukla perhaps, or Herman, or Charlene who was a Buddhist and lived in a Buddhist ashram. They would talk, and play the gramophone, and perhaps they would all cook up some sort of tasty lunch together on Maiska's little electric ring. But in the middle of these pleasant speculations, he suddenly remembered Lily and how she had said, 'Name them, name them!' Then it became a matter of pride not to go to Maiska's today. She was, he told himself, only one of many other possibilities, and today it so happened that he felt more like visiting one of his Indian friends. He remembered the names he had mentioned to Lily – Sri Manohar, Her Highness of Palangkot – all his good friends who would welcome him; though of course they were all busy, important people, and it was necessary to make an appointment first and pass through several secretaries. But, good heavens, there were others – many, many other good friends – whose doors were always open to him and who would be delighted to see him any time he cared to call.

* * *

Mrs. Chawla was not in a very good mood. She was to have had her singing lesson that morning, but her singing master had not turned up. Unfortunately this happened quite frequently, and every time it did, she thought of dispensing with his services. But when he came again the next time, she always forgave him very readily, for he had a charming smile and was altogether so young and debonair that it seemed no more than his due only to have to work when he felt like it. Still, meanwhile it was dull and disappointing not to have one's singing lesson when one had been looking forward to it; and after having scolded her servants on various points of disorder, she retired in a huff to her bedroom where she lay down on the floor and began to do her yogic exercises.

She was in the middle of the Sarvangasana and had got her legs laboriously into the air and was bending now one and now the other, when her servant knocked timidly on the door. 'No!' she called at once. 'I'm busy!'

When she heard, however, that a sahib had come and was waiting downstairs in the drawing-room, she became a little better pleased and got up and began to brush her hair before the mirror.

She entered the drawing-room with a smile. Dr. Ernst struggled instantly to his feet (not very easy, for Mrs. Chawla's décor was in true Indian style, with seats at floor-level). He noticed at once that the smile with which she entered grew stiff and uncordial when she saw that it was he. His heart sank – he had often been an unwelcome visitor – but it was too late to retreat. In an attempt to make her better pleased with him, he arched himself reverentially over her hand and brushed it with his lips; he knew that Indian ladies, though they pretended not to like it, were always flattered by this form of greeting. But today she was ungracious and withdrew her hand too quickly, and afterwards he saw her wipe it on the end of her sari.

He had learned long ago that the trouble with dropping in on people was that, unless they were as pleased to see him as he was to visit them, the atmosphere tended to be strained. He did his best: yet Mrs. Chawla took no trouble in return, only sat there and made no attempt to look anything but sulky and bored. He admired her so much; both for her appearance and her personality. She was a tall, proud woman with a fine bosom and a fine pair of fiery eyes; and she was very artistically inclined, a founder member of the Intimate Theatre Club and one of the principal organizers of the Indian Music Circle. One glimpse into her drawing-room revealed at once that she was a deeply cultured person, for it was full of wonderful artistic pieces such as a huge carved chest (once a village dowry chest but nowadays very fashionable in place of a sideboard), a heavy brass tray from Kashmir used as a coffee-table, a delightful old-fashioned urn and bowl made of copper, and a silver rose-water sprinkler. Sticks of incense smouldering from incense-holders gave a richly Indian smell and atmosphere to the room.

He had often before complimented her on the indigenous quality of her interior decoration; but when he did so today – as usual contrasting it favourably with the fashion of yesteryear when everyone had prided themselves on their imported sofa-suites and Axminster carpets – his compliments were not received as graciously as they usually were. On the contrary, she was even quite snappish:

'At last we are allowed to enjoy our own cultural heritage. Now that we are no longer under the heel of foreign imperialists'; and then she glared at him for a moment as if he too, poor Dr. Ernst, were or had ambitions to be a foreign imperialist.

He blushed and began to talk fast. He agreed with her heartily about the baneful influence that results from the forcible grafting of one culture on to another, and thence proceeded to eulogize all aspects of Indian art, architecture, music, dance, drama, food, dress, customs, and ceremonies. He went on and on, though she wasn't listening and he knew it; but he felt compelled to make it clear how completely he was on her side, on India's side. He longed to hear her say something encouraging in reply, to give him some assurance that she accepted his allegiance. The fact that she didn't, and his intuition that she wouldn't – never never would, however long he might be here and however passionately he might desire to identify himself – made him go on desperately talking. He looked at her with eyes that were soft and hurt and shamelessly appealing; and when she yawned, opening her mouth wide and half closing her beautiful passionate eyes, he longed to cry out, 'If only you knew how I love, how I admire you!' She lounged close to him on that silk-covered, floor-level seat. It was a little difficult for him to make himself comfortable, and he had to shift his legs from one side to the other; but she seemed to be perfectly at her ease, leaning with her elbow on the bolster behind her, one hip pushed out, and her large legs under the sari folded effortlessly beneath her. While his eyes never left her, she hardly glanced at him but lounged there inert and passive, now yawning, now putting her hand inside her low-cut blouse there lazily to scratch.

But suddenly she changed. She sat up, and all that inert mass throbbed with animation, and her sleepy eyes opened wide. She cried, 'So late!' and Dr. Ernst turned round to where she was looking and saw a young man with curly hair and a fine pair of shoulders. The young man was smiling in a relaxed way and said, 'Better late than never, I think.'

No one glanced at Dr. Ernst. Mrs. Chawla and the young man sat on the carpet, the young man with a small harmonium. She began to sing scales. 'Sa-ray-ga-ma-pa-da-ni-sa,' she sang, and he nodded, and she glanced at him, and he said, go on, go on, and made her do it over, while he kept on nodding. Finally she said, 'Oh I am tired of your scales!' and he said, 'You must obey your master.' Then she began to plead with him, so charming she was with him, putting on appealing little airs, pursing her mouth, lowering her eyes, plucking at the hem of her sari: but in such a way that one knew she wasn't really pleading, it was all a game only. That was the way he answered too, as if it were all a game and he was playing at being the severe singing-master, and they both seemed to enjoy themselves and wasted quite a lot of time, chatting back and forth. Dr. Ernst, too, smilingly put in a word, pleaded playfully for Mrs. Chawla to be allowed a song, but he was not heard.

At last, when she had begged enough, the singing-master gave way and allowed her to sing. It was one of those ambiguous devotional songs, where no one can be sure who is crying out to whom – the soul to God or the lover to the beloved. She tried to sing with feeling, but it was obvious that she did not have much talent. She sang slowly and stolidly, while the young man as stolidly accompanied her on the harmonium and made a resigned face. Dr. Ernst enjoyed the performance. He leaned forward eagerly, and there was a smile of delight on his face. Of course, he realized that she did not sing well, but it was not her singing that moved him so much as the picture she made. She and the young man together. They sat in the middle of the carpet which was floral in pattern and fresh and delicate as a meadow of flowers in a Moghul miniature; but the two figures – though they were grouped like lovers, close together, he with his instrument, she giving song – were not in the least delicate. They were solid and strong, he with his broad chest and his coarse, handsome face, and she with her large rounded limbs hidden but suggestively delineated by the folds of her sari; her full throat was flung back and emitted loud, lusty sounds. Their heads were close together and both richly covered with healthy, shining, blue-black hair.

When the song was finished, Dr. Ernst clapped in applause. 'Bravo!' he cried in his enthusiasm, and after that 'Encore!' just as if he were at the opera in Vienna. Mrs. Chawla for the first time turned her face and gave him a short, absent smile before turning back to the young man and telling him something in a low voice. He shrugged in resigned agreement and began to play the harmonium again, while she embarked on a second song. But she had not got very far when he broke off and made some criticism; he did this in an ungracious, almost contemptuous way, so that she stopped singing and her expression became sulky. They looked at each other in dislike. Dr. Ernst, hoping to make things better, said, 'To a layman's ear it sounded very nice,' but this did not have the desired effect. Instead Mrs. Chawla turned her look of dislike on him, her eyes blazed and she said, not to him but into the air, 'It is very difficult for me to concentrate on my singing when others are there to create a disturbance.'

Dr. Ernst saw it was time to go. He picked up his hat, got up and made his farewell bow, holding his hat against his navel as he did so. Once outside, he forced himself to be cheerful and walked briskly along. It was foolish, he told himself, to feel hurt or slighted. She had not meant anything personal – it was only that she was having her lesson, and of course no one wishes to be disturbed during a lesson. It was kind enough of her to have let him stay as long as she did. She was his good friend and esteemed and liked him as much as he did her. You silly old Ernst, he chided himself for having some feelings to the contrary; always so touchy, that was his trouble, looking for offence where none was meant. It was a very bad trait in him.

Sometimes during his morning peregrinations he was lucky and was offered lunch; today was not such a day. He entered a coffee-bar and carefully studied the menu. Actually he didn't have to do this for he frequented the place, and every other one like it, often enough to know that, beyond hamburgers, hot dogs, and vegetable cutlets, there would be nothing to tempt his palate. Yet every time he came he insisted on reading right through the menu – which had managed to get very dirty in spite of its cellophane covering – before giving his order. Perhaps there was the hope that some new dish had been added. Or perhaps because studying the menu was part of restaurant going, recalled days when one entered such places not solely for eating but for other, less tangible reasons as well: the way his parents had gone to restaurants, and he too, long ago. They had gone not because they had to but because they liked to once in a while, leaving their comfortable home and dressing up in going-out clothes, all of them on special behaviour, ready for an evening of elegance and entertainment.

The coffee-bar was a somewhat shabby one, though it had started off grandly enough with a moulded ceiling and crimson and gold cornices, but since the materials used had been of too cheap a quality, it did not take long for the place to get to its present peeling stage. The patrons, however, were not in the least shabby but very well and even flashily dressed in the latest California-style clothes to have reached the shops. Most of them were students or recent graduates, who had not yet taken up any burdens and were still comfortably looked after by rich and indulgent parents. They none of them seemed short of cash, casually ordering a succession of drinks and dishes which made Dr. Ernst, who was usually hungry, even hungrier; and there was certainly no shortage of twenty-five paise coins to put into the juke-box which played continuously, mostly last year's American hit-tunes, interspersed sometimes with the latest wailing, weepy Bombay film-song. At one time the juke-box had been a trial to Dr. Ernst, for it was loud and very shrill in a mechanical, tinny way; but now he had got used to it and even liked it and would have missed it if it had stopped. He had begun to recognize many of the tunes and to tap his feet to them the way the young men did; only of course he did it more decorously and with his feet hidden under the table.

He liked the place. He sat alone in a corner, eating his hamburger and shaking the bottle to get out some more of the congealed tomato ketchup; when he had finished, he liked simply sitting there and watching the other customers. He watched them with the same pleasure as he did Miss Jaya going off trimly to work in the morning, or Mrs.

Chawla and her music-teacher: admiring them for their youth, their vitality, the future that lay before them. None of them spoke to or took any notice of him; but he didn't expect them to. They were as infinitely above him, he felt with a not unhappy inward smile, as Lise Fruhlingsfeld; or as Lily's handsome young men were above Lily herself. They even looked, in comparison with Lily and himself, a higher kind of being, with their healthy, brown, glowing skins and their brilliant dark eyes and strong teeth and hair. How well they fitted in with everything: and here he thought not only of the coffee-bar with the loud juke-box and the crimson and gold mouldings but of everything that lay outside, the fast-growing creepers and flowers of too brilliant colours, the intensely blue skies, the birds and beasts that lived in jungles, the rivers, the vast mountain ranges – it all, all belonged to them and they to it, man and nature made to each other, where he and Lily and Maiska and Herman and the rest of them would always remain only pale, stray strangers.

Much as he liked being there, with the juke-box and the young men, he always found after a while – and this happened regularly – that a great oppression took hold of him. It was as if something too heavy, of which he could not bear the weight, had been laid on top of him. A ridiculous sensation, probably due to nothing more than the noise and the smoke; but all the same it was strong enough to make it necessary for him to leave. He paid his bill, leaving a tiny tip, and got up. Just as he reached the door, a new party of youths came surging in – a pride of bearded young Sikhs in flaming turbans and tartan shirts and expensive leather boots. Smiling, banging the juke-box, anticipating pleasure, they moved forward in a solid unseeing phalanx, so that Dr. Ernst, though lifting his hat and saying 'Excuse me, excuse me, please' without cease, was pushed back and could not reach the door. No one noticed him, and it was not till they had all found chairs for themselves and were drumming on the tables and shouting for the bearers that Dr. Ernst managed to regain the door and slip out into the street.

It was no longer pleasant outside. The day's heat had got into its stride and was white and electric sharp. Pariah dogs lay panting in little patches of shade, and from time to time a motor-car passed by, very swiftly, all its chromium burning and flashing white fire. Otherwise the streets were deserted, for the heat was a tyrant that strode the pavements and forced people to scuttle away to the nearest place of refuge.

* * *

Maiska's was not quite the nearest but it was near. Unfortunately Lily had got there before him, but for the time being he didn't even mind that, he was so glad to have arrived. He sat in one of the comfortable armchairs and shut his eyes for a moment, allowing heat and exhaustion to drain out of him. There was a kind of ache around his chest and stomach but that would pass off, he knew, it always did; all he needed was rest. The curtains were drawn in the room, so that everything was shrouded in a soothing dusk. Maiska and Lily were both lounging with their feet up on the settee, and it looked as if they had been there for a nice long comfortable time. They were both smoking Maiska's Egyptian cigarettes and drinking coffee out of thick pottery mugs painted in running colours. Records were scattered about on the floor near the record-player, which was open and still humming though the last record had finished playing.

Although he had meant to keep his eyes shut for only a moment, he found himself slipping more and more into a pleasant haze. He was vaguely aware of Maiska and Lily's voices talking together and the fan turning overhead and from the street a hawker calling digestive powders for sale and someone shouting on the stairs and someone else clattering up them with a bucket. When he woke, suddenly opening his eyes, he found Maiska looking at him. She smiled at him and he smiled weakly back and wanted more than anything to shut his eyes and go to sleep again. But he made an effort and sat up in the chair in which he had been drooping – a moment's uneasy thought: had his mouth fallen open? had he snored? he hated to be seen off guard, too privately – then took out his handkerchief and wiped it over his wet, perspiring face and neck and head. 'Must have dropped off,' he mumbled and smiled again at Maiska, apologetically.

She said, 'Go on, sleep a bit more.' She looked at him with sympathy and as if she knew just how tired he was and how he didn't want to wake up.

But he had to. Of course, a nap in the afternoon was nothing to reproach oneself with – good heavens, at his age and in this climate! – but one also had to know when to cut it short. Otherwise there was the danger of sinking too deep and giving way to the desire to sleep for ever and not have to get up at all any more and walk around and meet people. He put away his handkerchief and patted and jerked and brushed at his crumpled clothes to get them dapper again.

While he was doing this, he said, casually, not looking at Lily, 'I spent a very nice morning with Mrs. Chawla.'

'I can't stand her,' Lily said at once. 'A conceited stupid cow.'

'She asked me to come again very soon.' Then he shouted at Lily: 'Be careful how you speak of my friends!'

He was very angry, and it did him good. He shouted some more, and what a relief it was not to have to curb one's feelings for once but to be able to indulge them, relish a sense of one's own injury! No one tried to stop him and only when he had finished Lily said, quite mildly, 'I didn't know she was your friend.'

'You didn't know,' he repeated in exasperation. 'I told you: I have many, many Indian friends.'

He waited for this challenge to be taken up and was partly mollified when it wasn't. Maiska cleared a space on the table so as to be able to place a mug of coffee in front of him, into which she spooned sugar, murmuring to herself, 'Two and a half,' for she always knew exactly how much sugar each of her friends took and didn't have to ask.

Dr. Ernst was not very angry any more, but all the same he felt Lily shouldn't be let off too easily. He told her, 'Put your leg down,' for she was sitting in an easy but not decorous position. 'Aren't you ashamed? No wonder all your young men don't want to look at you.'

'Don't rub it in,' said Lily plaintively; at which Maiska laughed, but to cover up any tactlessness, she said, 'Never mind, one day she'll meet the right one.'

'But I have!' wailed Lily. 'They've all been right! It's always me who's wrong.'

Dr. Ernst inwardly agreed. She *was* wrong. He looked at her, not so much in distaste now as in pity, feeling sorry for her because her body was clumsy and her skin too flabby and white. She couldn't help this, poor thing; but why had she come here, why had she stayed here, in a country where man and nature both were colourful and lush and without pity? He thought of Mrs. Chawla, of the young Sikhs in their boots and tartan shirts, and leaned towards Lily quite tenderly. He gave a little tug at her skirt to make it cover her knees, and said in a smiling, paternal voice, 'That's better.'

Maiska was putting another record on her record-player. She did not have many records, and those she had were old and none too clear, but they were all only the highest classics. There was Brahms and Beethoven and Bach, and often her friends gathered for an informal musical evening. They had all spent last New Year's Eve like that – Maiska and Lily and Dr. Ernst and Charlene and the Linskys and Herman and Anna Shukla. Maiska had served beer and sandwiches and they had put on record after record, and though at first there had been some conversation, as the night wore on they grew silent and listened only to the music and each thought his own thoughts. At midnight they were playing the choral part of Beethoven's Ninth Symphony and they all got up and wished each other a Happy New Year. 'Freude Schöner Götterfunken' had sounded, loud if blurred and a little cracked, from the record-player, filling the room and their hearts, and one or two of them (Dr. Ernst among them) had had tears in their eyes.

He could not identify the record she had put on now, but it was some sort of flute concerto – graceful and happy, Mozart he suspected, though he didn't like to ask in case he was wrong. His foot tapped and his head nodded in time: it was much, much nicer than Mrs. Chawla's singing. Suddenly he felt proud and European and full of affection for Maiska and Lily, co-heirs with him of a wondrous heritage – Mozart! Versailles! Goethe's Weimar! Lily was smoking a cigarette, making the end of it red and wet with lipstick and puffing out too much smoke, and Maiska brought more coffee in a saucepan and refilled their mugs brim-full. Dr.

Ernst began to sing with the music, and not content with that – so gay did it make him feel – he got up and put his hands sideways to his face and crossed his feet at the ankles, and thus played an imaginary flute, swaying this side and that and, at particularly piercing moments, getting up on his toes as if to reach with the music up to heaven.

Miss Sahib

The entrance to the house in which Miss Tuhy lived was up a flight of stairs between a vegetable shop and a cigarette and cold-drink one. The stairs were always dirty, and so was the space around the doorway, with rotted bits of vegetable and empty cigarette packets trampled into the mud. Long practice had taught Miss Tuhy to step around this refuse, smilingly and without rancour, and as she did so she always nodded friendly greetings to the vegetable-seller and the cold-drink man, both of whom usually failed to notice her. Everyone in the neighbourhood had got used to her, for she had lived there, in that same house, for many years.

It was not the sort of place in which one would have expected to find an Englishwoman like Miss Tuhy, but the fact was, she was too poor to live anywhere else. She had nothing but her savings, and these, in spite of her very frugal way of life, could not last for ever; and of course there was always the vexed question of how long she would live. Once, in an uncharacteristically realistic moment, she had calculated that she could afford to go on for another five years, which would bring her up to sixty-five. That seemed fair enough to her, and she did not think she had the right to ask for more. However, most of the time these questions did not arise for she tended to be too engrossed in the present to allow fears of the future to disturb her peace of mind.

She was, by profession and by passionate inclination, a teacher, but she had not taught for many years. She had first come to India thirty years ago to take up a teaching post at a school for girls from the first families, and she had taught there and at various other places for as long as she had been allowed. She did it with enthusiasm, for she loved the country and her students. When Independence came and all the other English teachers went home, it never for a moment occurred to her to join them, and she went on teaching as if nothing had changed. And indeed, as far as she was concerned, nothing did change for a number of years, and it was only at the end of that time that it was discovered she was not sufficiently well qualified to go on teaching in an Indian high school. She bowed her head to this decision, for she knew she wasn't; not compared with all those clever Indian girls who held M.A. degrees in politics, philosophy, psychology, and economics. As a matter of fact, even though they turned out to be her usurpers, she was proud of these girls; for wasn't it she and those like her who had educated them and made them what they now were – sharp, emancipated, centuries ahead of their mothers and grandmothers? So it was not difficult for her to cede to them with a good grace, to enjoy her farewell party, cry a bit at the speeches, and receive with pride and a glow in her heart the silver model of the Taj Mahal which was presented to her as a token of appreciation. After that, she sailed for England – not because she in the least wanted to, but because it was what everyone seemed to expect of her.

She did not stay long. True, no one here said she was not well qualified enough to teach and she had no difficulty in getting a job; but she was not happy. It was not the same. She liked young people always, and so she liked the young people she was teaching here; but she could not love them the way she had loved her Indian pupils. She missed their playfulness, their affection, their sweetness – by comparison the English children struck her as being cool and distant. And not only the children but everyone she met, or only saw in streets and shops: they seemed a colder people somehow, politer perhaps and more considerate than the Indians among whom she had spent so many years, but without (so she put it to herself) *real love.* Even physically the English looked cold to her, with their damp white skins and pale blue eyes, and she longed again to be surrounded by those glowing coloured skins; and those eyes! the dark, large, liquid Indian eyes! and hair that sprang with such abundance from their heads. And besides the people, it was everything else as well. Everything was too dim, too cold. There was no sun, the grass was not green, the flowers not bright enough, and the rain that continually drizzled from a washrag sky was a poor substitute for the silver rivers that had come rushing in torrents out of immense, dark-blue, monsoon clouds.

So she and her savings returned, improvidently, to India. Everyone still remembered her and was glad to see her again but, once the first warm greetings were over, they were all too busy to have much time to spare for her. She didn't mind, she was just happy to be back; and in any case she had to live rather a long way away from her friends because, now that she had no job, she had to be where rents were cheaper. She found the room in the house between the vegetable-seller and the cold-drink shop and lived there contentedly all the week round, only venturing forth on Sundays to visit her former colleagues and pupils. As time went on, these Sunday visits became fewer and further between, for everyone always seemed to be rather busy; anyway, there was less to say now, and also she found it was not always easy to spare the bus-fare to and fro. But it didn't matter, she was even happier staying at home because all her life was there now, and the interest and affection she had formerly bestowed on her colleagues and pupils, she now had as strongly for the other people living in the house, and even for the vegetable-seller and the cold-drink man though her contact with them never went further than smiles and nods.

The house was old, dirty, and inward-looking. In the centre was a courtyard which could be overlooked like a stage from the galleries running all the way round the upper storeys. The house belonged to an old woman who lived on the ground floor with her enormous family of children and grandchildren; the upper floors had been subdivided and let out to various tenants. The stairs and galleries were always crowded, not only with the tenants themselves but with their servants. Everyone in the house except Miss Tuhy kept a servant, a hill-boy, who cleaned and washed and cooked and was frequently beaten and frequently dismissed. There seemed to be an unending supply of these boys; they could be had very cheaply, and slept curled up on the stairs or on a threshold, and ate what was left in the pot.

Miss Tuhy was a shy person who loved other people but found it difficult to make contact with them. On the second floor lived an Anglo-Indian nurse with her grown-up son, and she often sought Miss Tuhy out, to talk in English with her, to ask questions about England, to discuss her problems and those of her son (a rather insipid young man who worked in an airlines office). She felt that she and Miss Tuhy should present a united front against the other neighbours, who were all Hindus and whom she regarded with contempt. But Miss Tuhy did not feel that way. She liked and was interested in everyone, and it seemed a privilege to her to be near them and to be aware of what seemed to her their fascinating, their passionate lives.

Down in the courtyard the old landlady ruled her family with a rod of iron. She kept a tight hold of everything and doled out little sums of pocket-money to her forty-year-old sons. She could often be heard abusing them and their wives, and sometimes she beat them. There was only one person to whom she showed any indulgence – who, in fact, could get away with anything – and that was Sharmila, one of her granddaughters. When Miss Tuhy first came to live in the house, Sharmila was a high-spirited, slapdash girl of twelve, with big black eyes and a rapidly developing figure. Although she had reached the age at which her sisters and cousins were already beginning to observe that reticence which, as grown women, would keep them away from the eyes of strangers, Sharmila still behaved with all the freedom of the smaller children, running round the courtyard and up and down the stairs and in and out of the homes of her grandmother's tenants. She was the first in the house to establish contact with Miss Tuhy, simply by bursting into the room where the English lady lived and looking round and touching things and lifting them up to examine them – 'What's that?' – all Miss Tuhy's treasures: her mother-of-pearl pen-holder, the photograph of her little niece as a bridesmaid, the silver Taj Mahal. Decorating the mantelpiece was a bowl of realistically shaped fruits made of plaster-of-paris, and before leaving Sharmila lifted a brightly-coloured banana out of the bowl and held it up and said, 'Can I have it?' After that she came every day, and every day, just before leaving, helped herself to one more fruit until they were all finished and then she took the bowl.

Sharmila was lazy at school all the year round, but she

always panicked before her class-promotion exams and came running for help to Miss Tuhy. These were Miss Tuhy's happiest times, for not only was she once again engaged in the happy pursuit of teaching, but she also had Sharmila sitting there with her all day long, bent ardently over her books and biting the tip of her tongue in her eagerness to learn. Miss Tuhy would have dearly loved to teach her the whole year round, and to teach her everything she knew, and with that end in view she had drawn up an ambitious programme for Sharmila to follow; but although sometimes the girl consented to submit to this programme, it was evident that once the terror of exams was past her interest sharply declined, so that sometimes, when Miss Tuhy looked up from a passionate reading of the romantic poets, she found her pupil fiddling with the strands of hair which always managed to escape from her sober pigtail and her mouth wide open in a yawn she saw no reason to disguise. And indeed Miss Tuhy had finally to admit that Sharmila was right; for what use would all this learning ever be to her when her one purpose in life, her sole duty, was to be married and give satisfaction to the husband who would be chosen for her and to the in-laws in whose house she would be sent to live?

She was just sixteen when she was married. Her grandmother, who usually hated spending money, excelled herself that time and it was a grand and memorable occasion. A big wedding marquee was set up in the courtyard and crammed tight with wedding-guests shimmering in their best clothes; all the tenants were invited too, including Miss Tuhy in her good dress (white dots on a chocolate brown background) and coral necklace. Like everyone else, she was excitedly awaiting the arrival of the bridegroom and his party. She wondered what sort of a boy they had chosen for her Sharmila. She wanted a tall, bold boy for her, a soldier and a hero; and she had heightened, almost mythological visions of the young couple – decked out in jewels and gorgeous clothes – gaily disporting themselves in a garden full of brightly-coloured flowers. But when at last the band accompanying the bridegroom's party was heard, and everyone shouted 'They have come!' and rushed to the entrance to get the first glimpse, then the figure that descended from the horse amid the jubilation of the trumpets was not, in spite of his garlands and his golden coat, a romantic one. Not only was Sharmila's bridegroom stocky and ill at ease, but he was also no longer very young. Miss Tuhy, who had fought her way to the front with the best of them, turned away in bitter disappointment. There were tears in her eyes. She knew it would not turn out well.

Sharmila came every day to visit her old home. At first she came in order to boast, to show off the saris and shawls and jewellery presented to her on her marriage, and to tell about her strange new life and the house she lived in and all her new family. She was brimming over with excitement and talked non-stop and danced round the courtyard. Some time later she came with different stories, about what her mother-in-law had said to her and what she had answered back, about her sisters-in-law and all the other women, how they tried to get the better of her but how she soon showed them a trick or two: she tucked in her chin and talked in a loud voice and was full of energy and indignation. Sometimes she stayed for several days and did not return till her husband came to coax her back. After a year the first baby arrived, and a year later the second, and after a few more years a third. Sharmila became fat and matronly, and her voice was louder and more raucous. She still came constantly, now with two of the children trailing behind her and a third riding on her hip, and she stayed longer than before, often refusing to go back even when her husband came to plead with her. And in the end she seemed to be there all the time, she and her children, so that, although nothing much was said on the subject, it was generally assumed that she had left her husband and her in-laws' house and had come back to live with her grandmother.

She was a little heavy now to go running up and down the stairs the way she used to: but she still came up to Miss Tuhy's room, and the English lady's heart still beat in the same way when she heard her step on the stair, though it was a different step now, heavier, slower, and accompanied by children's tiny shuffle and patter. 'Miss Sahib!' Sharmila would call from the landing, and Miss Tuhy would fling her door wide open and stand there beaming. Now it was the children who moved from object to object, touching everything and asking to know what it was, while Sharmila, panting a little from her climb up the stairs, flung herself on the narrow bed and allowed Miss Tuhy to tuck a pillow behind her back. When the children had examined all the treasures, they began to play their own games, they crawled all over the floor and made a lot of noise. Their mother lay on the bed and sometimes she laughed and sometimes she sighed and talked about everything that came into her head. They always stayed for several hours, and when they left at last, Miss Tuhy, gorged with bliss, shut the door and carefully cleaned out her little room which the children had so delightfully disordered.

When she didn't feel like going upstairs, Sharmila stood in the middle of the courtyard and shouted 'Miss Sahib!' in her loud voice. Miss Tuhy hurried downstairs, smoothing her dress and adjusting her glasses. She sat with Sharmila in the courtyard and helped her to shell peas. The old grandmother watched them from her bed inside the room: that terrible old woman was bedridden now and quite unable to move, a huge helpless shipwreck wrapped in shawls and blankets. Her speech was blurred and could be understood only by Sharmila who had become her interpreter and chief functionary. It was Sharmila, not one of the older women of the household, who carried the keys and distributed the stores and knew where the money was kept. While she sat with Miss Tuhy in the courtyard, every now and again the grandmother would make calling noises and then Sharmila would get up and go in to see what she wanted. Inside the room it was dark and smelled of sickness and old age, and Sharmila was glad to come out in the open again.

'Poor old Granny,' she said to Miss Tuhy, who nodded and also looked sad for Granny because she was old and bedridden: as for herself, she did not feel old at all but a young girl, sitting here like this shelling peas and chatting with Sharmila. The children played and sang, the sun shone, along the galleries upstairs the tenants went to and fro hanging out their washing; there was the sound of voices calling and of water running, traffic passed up and down on the road outside, a near-by flour-mill chucked and chucked. 'Poor old Granny,' Sharmila said again. 'When she was young, she was like a queen – tall, beautiful, everyone did what she wanted. If they didn't she stamped her foot and screamed and waved her arms in the air – like this,' Sharmila demonstrated, flailing her plump arms with bangles up to the elbow and laughing. But then she grew serious and put her face closer to Miss Tuhy's and said in a low, excited voice: 'They say she had a lover, a jeweller from Dariba. He came at nights when everyone was asleep and she opened the door for him.' Miss Tuhy blushed and her heart beat faster; though she tried to check them, a thousand impressions rippled over her mind.

'They say she was a lot like me,' said Sharmila, smiling a little and her eyes hazy with thought. She had beautiful eyes, very large and dark with heavy brows above them; her lips were full and her cheeks plump and healthy. When she was thoughtful or serious, she had a habit of tucking in her chin so that several chins were formed, and this too somehow was attractive, especially as these chins seemed to merge and swell into her very large, tight bust.

But her smile became a frown, and she said, 'Yes, and now look at her, how she is. Three times a day I have to change the sheets under her. This is the way it all ends. Hai,' and she heaved a sigh and a brooding look came on her face. The children, who had been chasing each other round the courtyard, suddenly began to quarrel in loud voices; at that Sharmila sprang up in a rage and caught hold of the biggest child and began to beat him with her fist, but hardly had he uttered the first cry when she stopped and instead lifted him in her arms and held him close, close to her bosom, her eyes shut in rapturous possessiveness as if he were all that she had.

It was one of the other tenants who told Miss Tuhy that Sharmila was having an affair with the son of the Anglo-Indian nurse from upstairs. The tenant told it with a lot of smiles, comments, and gestures, but Miss Tuhy pretended not to understand, she only smiled back at the informer in her gentle way and said 'Good morning', in English and shut the door of her room. She was very much excited. She thought about the young man whom she had seen often and sometimes talked to: a rather colourless young man, with brown hair and Anglo-Indian features, who always dressed in English clothes and played cricket on Sunday mornings. It seemed impossible to connect him in any way with Sharmila; and how his mother would have hated any such connection! The nurse, fully opening her heart to Miss Tuhy, never tired of expressing her contempt for the other tenants in the house who could not speak English and also did not know how to live decently. She and her son lived very decently, they had chairs and a table in their room and linoleum on the floor and a picture of the Queen of England on the wall. They ate with knife and fork. 'Those others, Miss Tuhy, I wouldn't like you to see,' she said with pinched lips (she was a thin woman with matchstick legs and always wore brown shoes and stockings). 'The dirt. Squalor. You would feel sick, Miss Tuhy. And the worst are those downstairs, the —' and she added a bad word in Hindi (she never said any bad words in English, perhaps she didn't know any). She hated Sharmila and the grandmother and that whole family. But she was often away on night-duty, and then who knew – as the other tenant had hinted – what went on?

Miss Tuhy never slept too well at nights. She often got up and walked round her room and wished it were time to light the fire and make her cup of tea. Those night hours seemed very long, and sometimes, tired of her room, she would go out on the stairs and along the galleries overlooking the courtyard. How silent it was now with everyone asleep! The galleries and the courtyard, so crowded during the day, were empty except where here and there a servant-boy lay sleeping huddled in a corner. There was no traffic on the road outside and the flour-mill was silent. Only the sky seemed alive, with the moon sliding slowly in and out of patches of mist. Miss Tuhy thought about the grandmother and the jeweller for whom she had opened the door when it was like this silent and empty at nights. She remembered conversations she had heard years ago among her English fellow-teachers. They had always had a lot to say about sensuality in the East. They whispered to each other how some of the older boys were seen in the town entering certain disreputable alleys, while boys who came from princely or landowner families were taught everything there was to know by women on their fathers' estates. And as for the girls – well, they whispered, one had only to look at them, how quickly they ripened: could one ever imagine an English girl so developed at thirteen? It was, they said, the climate; and of course the food they ate, all those curries and spices that heated the blood. Miss Tuhy wondered: if she had been born in India, had grown up under this sun and had eaten the food, would she have been different? Instead of her thin, inadequate, English body, would she have grown up like the grandmother who had opened the door to the jeweller, or like Sharmila with flashing black eyes and a big bust?

Nothing stirred, not a sound from anywhere, as if all those lively people in the house were dead. Miss Tuhy stared and stared down at Sharmila's door and the courtyard washed in moonlight, and wondered was there a secret, was something going on that should not be? She crept along the gallery and up the stairs towards the nurse's door. Here too everything was locked and silent, and if there was a secret, it was being kept. She put her ear to the door and stayed there, listening. She did not feel in the least bad or guilty doing this, for what she wanted was nothing for herself but only to have proof that Sharmila was happy.

She did not seem happy. She was getting very bad-tempered and was for ever fighting with her family or with the other tenants. It was a not uncommon sight to have her standing in the middle of the courtyard, arms akimbo, keys at her waist, shouting insults in her loud, somewhat raucous voice. She no longer came to visit Miss Tuhy in her room, and once, when the English lady came to be with her downstairs, she shouted at her that she had enough with one old woman on her hands and did not have time for any more. But that night she came upstairs and brought a little dish of carrot halwa which Miss Tuhy tried to refuse, turning her face away and saying primly that thank you, she was not hungry. 'Are you angry with me, Missie Sahib?' coaxed Sharmila with a smile in her voice, and she dug her forefinger into the halwa and then brought it to Miss Tuhy's lips, saying 'One little lick, just one, for Sharmila', till Miss Tuhy put out her tongue and shyly slid it along Sharmila's finger. She blushed as she did so, and anger and hurt melted out of her heart.

'There!' cried Sharmila, and then she flung herself as usual on the bed. She began to talk, to unburden herself completely. Tears poured down her cheeks as she spoke of her unhappy life and all the troubles brought down upon her by the grandmother who did not give her enough money and treated her like a slave, the other family members who were jealous of her, the servants who stole from her, the shopkeepers who cheated her – 'If it weren't for my children,' she cried, 'why should I go on? I'd make an end of it and get some peace at last.'

'Sh,' said Miss Tuhy, shocked and afraid.

'Why not? What have I got to live for?'

'*You?*' said Miss Tuhy with an incredulous laugh, and looked at that large, full-bloomed figure sprawled there on the narrow bed and rumpling the bedcover from which the embroidery (girls carrying baskets of apples and pansies on their arms) had almost completely faded.

Sharmila said, 'Did I ever tell you about that woman, two doors away from the coal-merchant's house? She was a widow and they treated her like a dog, so one night she took a scarf and hung herself from a hook on the stairs. We all went to have a look at her. Her feet were swinging in the air as if there was a wind blowing. I was only four but I still remember.'

There was an eerie little pause which Miss Tuhy broke as briskly as she could: 'What's the matter with you? A young woman like you with all your life before you – I wonder you're not ashamed.'

'I want to get away from here! I'm so sick of this *house*!'

'Yes, Miss Tuhy,' said the Anglo-Indian nurse a few days later, when the English lady had come to pay her a visit and they both sat drinking tea under the tinted portrait of the Queen, 'I'm just sick and tired of living here, that I can tell you. If I could get out tomorrow, I would. But it's not so easy to find a place, not these days with the rents.' She sighed and poured the two of them strong tea out of an earthenware pot. She drank in as refined a way as Miss Tuhy, without making any noise at all. 'My boy's wanting to go to England, and why not? No future for us here, not with these people.'

Miss Tuhy gave a hitch to her wire-framed glasses and smiled ingratiatingly: 'No young lady for him yet?' she asked, and her voice quavered like an inefficient spy's.

'Oh, he goes with the odd girl or two. Nothing serious. There's time yet. We're not like those others – hurry-curry, muddle-puddle, marry them off at sixteen, and they never even see each other's face! No wonder there's trouble afterwards.' She put her bony brown hand on Miss Tuhy's knee and brought her face close: 'Like that one downstairs, the she-devil. It's so disgusting. I don't even like to tell you.' But her tongue was already wiping round her pale lips in anticipation of the telling.

Miss Tuhy got up abruptly. She dared not listen, and for some unknown reason tears had sprung into her eyes. She went out quickly but the nurse followed her. It was dark on the stairs and Miss Tuhy's tears could not be seen. The nurse clung to her arm: 'With servants,' she whispered into Miss Tuhy's ear. 'She gets them in at night when everyone's asleep. Mary Mother,' said the nurse and crossed herself. Instantly a quotation rose to Miss Tuhy's lips: 'Her sins are forgiven, for she loved much. But to whom little is forgiven, the same loveth little.' The nurse was silent for a moment and then she said, '*She*'s not Christian,' with contempt. Miss Tuhy freed her arm and hurried to her own room. She sat in her chair with her hands folded in her lap and her legs trembling. A procession of servants filed through her mind: undersized hill-boys with naked feet and torn shirts, sickly but tough, bent on survival. She heard their voices as they called to each other in their weird hill-accents and laughed with each other, showing pointed teeth. Every few years one of them in the neighbourhood went berserk and murdered his master and ran away with the jewellery and cash, only to be caught the next day on a wild spree at cinemas and country liquor shops. Strange wild boys, wolf-boys: Miss Tuhy had always liked them and felt sorry for them. But now she felt most sorry for Sharmila, and prayed for it not to be true.

It could not be true. Sharmila had such an innocent nature. She was a child. She loved sweet things to eat, and when the bangle-seller came, she was the first to run to meet him. She was also very fond of going to the cinema, and when she came home she told Miss Tuhy the story. She acted out all the more important scenes, especially the love-scenes – 'Just as their lips were about to meet, quick as a flash, with her veil flying in the wind, she ran to the next tree and called to him – Arjun! – and he followed her and he put his arms round the tree and this time she did not run away – no, they stood looking at each other, eating each other up with their eyes, and then the music – oh, Missie, Missie, Missie!' she would end and stretch her arms into the air and laugh with longing.

Once, on her little daily shopping trip to the bazaar, Miss Tuhy caught sight of Sharmila in the distance. And seeing her like that, unexpectedly, she saw her as a stranger might, and realized for the first time that the Sharmila she knew no longer existed. Her image of Sharmila was two-fold, one superimposed on the other yet also simultaneous, the two images merged in her mind: there was the hoyden schoolgirl, traces of whom still existed in her smile and in certain glances of her eyes, and then there was Sharmila in bloom, the young wife dancing round the courtyard and boasting about her wedding presents. But the woman she now saw in the bazaar was fat and slovenly; the end of her veil, draped carelessly over her breasts, trailed a little in the dust, and the heel of her slipper was trodden over to one side so that she seemed to be dragging her foot when she walked. She was quarrelling with one of the shopkeepers, she was gesticulating and using coarse language; the other shopkeepers leaned out of their stalls to listen, and from the way they grinned and commented to each other, it was obvious that Sharmila was a well-known figure and the scene she was enacting was one she had often played before. Miss Tuhy, in pain, turned and walked away in the opposite direction, even though it meant a longer way home. For the first time she failed to greet the vegetable-seller and the cold-drink man as she passed between their two shops on her way into the house, and when she had to step round the refuse trodden into the mud, she felt a movement of distaste and thought irritably to herself why it was that no one ever took the trouble to clean the place. The stairs of the house too were dirty, and there was a bad smell of sewage. She reached her room with a sigh of relief, but it seemed as if the bad smell came seeping in from under the closed door. Then she heard again Sharmila's anguished voice crying, 'I want to get away! I'm so sick of this *house*!' and she too felt the same anguish to get away from the house and from the streets and crowded bazaars around it.

That night she said to Sharmila, in a bright voice, 'Why don't we all go away somewhere for a lovely holiday?'

Sharmila, who had never had occasion to leave the city she was born in, thought it was a joke and laughed. But Miss Tuhy was very much in earnest. She remembered all the holidays she had gone on years ago when she was still teaching. She had always gone to the Simla hills and stayed in an English boarding-house, and she had taken long walks every day and breathed in the mountain air and collected pine cones. She told Sharmila all about this, and Sharmila too began to get excited and said, 'Let's go', and asked many more questions.

'Sausages and bacon for breakfast every morning,' Miss Tuhy reminisced, and Sharmila, who had never eaten either, clapped her hands with pleasure and gave an affectionate squeeze to her youngest child playing in her lap: 'You'll like that, Munni, na? Shaushage? Hmmm!'

'They'll get wonderful red cheeks up there,' said Miss Tuhy, 'real English apple cheeks,' and she smiled at the sallow city-child dressed in dirty velvet. 'And there'll be pony-rides and wild flowers to pick and lovely cool water from the mountain streams.'

'Let's go!' cried Sharmila with another hug to her child.

'We'll go by train,' said Miss Tuhy. 'And then a bus'll take us up the mountains.'

Sharmila suddenly stopped smiling: 'Yes, and the money? Where's that to come from? You think *she*'d ever give?' and she tossed her head towards the room where her grandmother lay, immobile and groaning but still a power to be reckoned with.

Miss Tuhy waved her aside: 'This'll be *my* treat,' she said.

And why not? The money was there, and what pleasure it would be to spend it on a holiday with Sharmila and the children! She brutally stifled all thoughts of caution, of the future. Money was there to be spent, to take pleasure with, not to eke out a miserable day by day existence which, in any case, might end – who knew? – tomorrow or the day after. And then what use would it ever be to her? Her glasses slipped and lay crooked on her nose, her face was flushed: she looked drunk with excitement. 'You'll get such a surprise,' she said. 'When we're sitting in the bus, and it's going up up up, higher and higher, and you'll see the mountains before you, more beautiful than anything you've ever dreamed of.'

Unfortunately Sharmila and the children were all very sick in the bus that carried them up the mountains, and so could not enjoy the scenery. Sharmila, in between retching with abandon, wept loudly that she was dying and cursed the fate that had brought her here instead of leaving her quietly at home where she belonged and was happy. However, once the bus had stopped and they had reached their destination, they began to enjoy themselves. They were amused by the English boarding-house, and at meal-times were lost in wonder not only at the food, the like of which they had never eaten, but also at the tablecloths and the cutlery. Their first walk was undertaken with great enthusiasm, and they collected everything they found on the way – pine cones and flowers and leaves and stones and empty cigarette packets. As Miss Tuhy had promised, they rode on ponies: even Sharmila, gasping and giggling and letting out loud cries of fright, was hoisted on to the back of a pony but had to be helped down again, dissolving in fits of laughter, because she was too heavy. Miss Tuhy revelled in their enjoyment; and for herself she was happy too to be here again among the familiar smells of pine and wood-fires and cold air. She loved the pale mists that rose from the mountainside and the rain that rained down so softly. She wished they could stay for ever. But after the third day Sharmila and the children began to get bored and kept asking when they were going home. They no longer cared to go for walks or ride on ponies. When it rained, all four of them sat mournfully by the window, and sighed and moaned and kept asking, what shall we do now? and Sharmila wondered how human beings could bear to live in a place like this; speaking for herself, it was just the same as being dead. Miss Tuhy had to listen not only to their complaints but also to those of the management, for Sharmila and the children were behaving badly – especially in the dining-room where, after the third day, they began demanding pickles and chapattis, and the children spat out the unfamiliar food on the tablecloth while Sharmila abused the hotel servants in bazaar language.

So they went home again earlier than they had intended. They had been away less than ten days, but their excitement on seeing the old places again was that of long-time voyagers. They had hired a tonga at the station and, as they neared home, they began to point out familiar landmarks to each other; by the time they had got to their own neighbourhood bazaar, the children were bobbing up and down so much that they were in danger of falling off the carriage, and Sharmila shouted cordial greetings to the shopkeepers with whom she would be fighting again tomorrow. And at home all the relatives and friends crowded into the courtyard to receive them, and there was much kissing and embracing and even a happy tear or two, and the tenants and servants thronged the galleries upstairs to watch the scene and call down their welcome to the travellers. It was a great homecoming.

Only Miss Tuhy was not happy. She did not want to be back. She longed now for the green mountains and the clean, cool air; she also missed the boarding-house with its English landlady and very clean stairs and bathrooms. It was intensely hot in the city and dust-storms were blowing. The sky was covered with an ugly yellow heat haze, and all day hot, restless winds blew dust about. Loudspeaker vans were driven through the streets to advise people to be vaccinated against the current outbreak of smallpox. Miss Tuhy hardly left her room. She felt ill and weak, and contrary to her usual custom, she often lay down on her bed, even during the day. She kept her doors and windows shut, but nevertheless the dust seeped in, and so did the smells and the noise of the house. She no longer went on her daily shopping and preferred not to eat. Sharmila brought food up for her, but Miss Tuhy did not want it, it was too spicy for her and too greasy. 'Just a little taste,' Sharmila begged and brought a morsel to her lips. Miss Tuhy pushed her hand away and cried out, 'Go away!

I can't stand the smell!' She meant not only the smell of the food, but also that of Sharmila's heavy, perspiring body.

It was in these days of terrible heat that the grandmother at last managed to die. Miss Tuhy dragged herself up from her bed in order to attend the funeral on the bank of the river. It was during the hottest part of the day, and the sun spread such a pall of white heat that, seen through it, the flames of the pyre looked colourless and quite harmless as they first licked and then rose higher and enveloped the body of the grandmother. The priest chanted and the eldest son poured clarified butter to feed the fire. All the relatives shrieked and wailed and beat their thighs in the traditional manner. Sharmila shrieked the loudest – she tore open her breast and, beating it with her fists, demanded to be allowed to die, and then she tried to fling herself on the pyre and had to be held back by four people. Vultures swayed overhead in the dust-laden sky. The river had dried up and the sand burned underfoot. Everything was white, desolate, empty, for miles and miles and miles around, on earth and, apart from the vultures, in the sky. Sharmila suddenly flung herself on Miss Tuhy and held her in a stifling embrace. She wept that now only she, Miss Tuhy, was left to her, and promised to look after her and tend and care for her as she had done for her dear, dead granny. Miss Tuhy gasped for air and tried to free herself, but Sharmila only clung to her the tighter and her tears fell on and smeared Miss Tuhy's cheeks.

Miss Tuhy's mother had died almost forty years ago, but Miss Tuhy could still vividly recall her funeral. It had drizzled, and rich smells of damp earth had mixed with the more delicate smell of tuberoses and yew. The clergyman's words brought ease and comfort, and weeping was restrained; birds sang cheerfully from out of the wet trees. That's the way to die, thought Miss Tuhy, and bitterness welled up into her hitherto gentle heart. The trouble was, she no longer had the fare home to England, not even on the cheapest route.

The Man with the Dog

I think of myself sometimes as I was in the early days, and I see myself moving around my husband's house the way I used to do: freshly bathed, flowers in my hair, I go from room to room and look in corners to see that everything is clean. I walk proudly. I know myself to be loved and respected as one who faithfully fulfils all her duties in life – towards God, parents, husband, children, servants, and the poor. When I pass the prayer-room, I join my hands and bow my head and sweet reverence flows in me from top to toe. I know my prayers to be pleasing and acceptable.

Perhaps it is because they remember me as I was in those days that my children get so angry with me every time they see me now. They are all grown up now and scattered in many parts of India. When they need me, or when my longing for them becomes too strong, I go and visit one or other of them. What happiness! They crowd round me, I kiss them and hug them and cry, I laugh with joy at everything my little grandchildren say and do, we talk all night there is so much to tell. As the days pass, however, we touch on other topics that are not so pleasant, or even if we don't touch on them, they are there and we think of them, and our happiness becomes clouded. I feel guilty and, worse, I begin to feel restless, and the more restless I am the more guilty I feel. I want to go home, though I dare not admit it to them. At the same time I want to stay, I don't ever ever want to leave them – my darling beloved children and grandchildren for whom what happiness it would be to lay down my life! But I have to go, the restlessness is burning me up, and I begin to tell them lies. I say that some urgent matter has come up and I have to consult my lawyer. Of course, they know it is lies, and they argue with me and quarrel and say things that children should not have to say to their mother; so that when at last I have my way and my bags are packed, our grief is more than only that of parting. All the way home, tears stream down my cheeks and my feelings are in turmoil, as the train carries me farther and farther away from them, although it is carrying me towards that which I have been hungering and burning for all the time I was with them.

Yes, I, an old woman, a grandmother many times over – I hunger and burn! And for whom? For an old man. And having said that, I feel like throwing my hands before my face and laughing out loud, although of course it may happen, as it often does to me nowadays, that my laughter will change into sobs and then back again as I think of him, of that old man whom I love so much. And how he would hate it, to be called an old man! Again I laugh when I think of his face if he could hear me call him that. The furthest he has got is to think of himself as middle-aged. Only the other day I heard him say to one of his lady-friends, 'Yes, now that we're all middle-aged, we have to take things a bit more slowly'; and he stroked his hand over his hair, which he combs very carefully so that the bald patches don't show, and looked sad because he was middle-aged.

I think of the first time I ever saw him. I remember everything exactly. I had been to Spitzer's to buy some little Swiss cakes, and Ram Lal, who was already my chauffeur in those days, had started the car and was just taking it out of its parking space when he drove straight into the rear bumper of a car that was backing into the adjacent space. This car was not very grand, but the Sahib who got out of it was. He wore a beautifully tailored suit with creases in the trousers and a silk tie and a hat on his head; under his arm he carried a vary hairy little dog, which was barking furiously. The Sahib too was barking furiously, his face had gone red all over and he shouted abuses at Ram Lal in English. He didn't see me for a while, but when he did he suddenly stopped shouting, almost in the middle of a word. He looked at me as I sat in the back of the Packard in my turquoise sari and a cape made out of an embroidered Kashmiri shawl; even the dog stopped barking. I knew that look well. It was one that men had given me from the time I was fifteen right till – yes, even till I was over forty. It was a look that always filled me with annoyance but also (now that I am so old I can admit it) pride and pleasure. Then, a few seconds later, still looking at me in the same way but by this time with a little smile as well, he raised his hat to me; his hair was blond and thin. I inclined my head, settled my cape around my shoulders, and told Ram Lal to drive on.

In those days I was very pleasure-loving. Children were all quite big, three of them were already in college and the two younger ones at their boarding-schools. When they were small and my dear husband was still with us, we lived mostly in the hills or on our estate near X – (which now belongs to my eldest son, Shammi); these were quiet, dull places where my dear husband could do all his reading, invite his friends, and listen to music. Our town house was let out in those years, and when we came to see his lawyer or consult some special doctor, we had to stay in a hotel. But after I was left alone and the children were bigger, I kept the town house for myself, because I liked living in town best. I spent a lot of time shopping and bought many costly saris that I did not need; at least twice a week I visited a cinema and I even learned to play cards! I was invited to many tea parties, dinners, and other functions.

It was at one of these that I met him again. We recognized each other at once, and he looked at me in the same way as before, and soon we were making conversation. Now that we are what we are to each other and have been so for all these years, it is difficult for me to look back and see him as I did at the beginning – as a stranger with a stranger's face and a stranger's name. What interested me in him the most at the beginning was, I think, that he was a foreigner; at the time I hadn't met many foreigners, and I was fascinated by so many things about him that seemed strange and wonderful to me. I liked the elegant way he dressed, and the lively way in which he spoke, and his thin fair hair, and the way his face would go red. I was also fascinated by the way he talked to me and to the other ladies: so different from our Indian men who are always a little shy with us and clumsy, and even if they like to talk with us, they don't want anyone to see that they like it. But he didn't care who saw – he would sit on a little stool by the side of the lady with whom he was talking, and he would look up at her and smile and make conversation in a very lively manner, and sometimes, in talking, he would lay his hand on her arm. He was also extra polite with us, he drew back the chair for us when we wanted to sit down or get up, and he would open the door for us, and he lit the cigarettes of those ladies who smoked, and all sorts of other little services which our Indian men would be ashamed of and think beneath their dignity. But the way he did it all, it was full of dignity. And one other thing, when he greeted a lady and wanted her to know that he thought highly of her, he would kiss her hand, and this too was beautiful, although the first time he did it to me

I had a shock like electricity going down my spine and I wanted to snatch away my hand from him and wipe it clean on my sari. But afterwards I got used to it and I liked it.

His name is Boekelman, he is a Dutchman, and when I first met him he had already been in India for many years. He had come out to do business here, in ivory, and was caught by the war and couldn't get back; and when the war was over, he no longer wanted to go back. He did not earn a big fortune, but it was enough for him. He lived in a hotel suite which he had furnished with his own carpets and pictures, he ate well, he drank well, he had his circle of friends, and a little hairy dog called Susi. At home in Holland all he had left were two aunts and a wife, from whom he was divorced and whom he did not even like to think about (her name was Annemarie, but he always spoke of her as 'Once bitten, twice shy'). So India was home for him, although he had not learned any Hindi except 'achchha' which means all right and 'pani' which means water, and he did not know any Indians. All his friends were foreigners; his lady-friends also.

Many things have changed now from what they were when I first knew him. He no longer opens the door for me to go in or out, nor does he kiss my hand; he still does it for other ladies, but no longer for me. That's all right, I don't want it, it is not needed. We live in the same house now, for he has given up his hotel room and has moved into a suite of rooms in my house. He pays rent for this, which I don't want but can't refuse, because he insists; and anyway, perhaps it doesn't matter, because it isn't very much money (he has calculated the rent not on the basis of what would have to be paid today but on what it was worth when the house was first built, almost forty years ago). In return, he wishes to have those rooms kept quite separate and that everyone should knock before they go in; he also sometimes give parties in there for his European friends, to which he may or may not invite me. If he invites me, he will do it like this: 'One or two people are dropping in this evening, I wonder if you would care to join us?' Of course I have known long before this about the party, because he has told the cook to get something ready, and the cook has come to me to ask what should be made, and I have given full instructions; if something very special is needed, I make it myself. After he has invited me and I have accepted, the next thing he asks me, 'What will you wear?' and he looks at me very critically. He always says women must be elegant, and that was why he first liked me, because in those days I was very careful about my appearance, I bought many new saris and had blouses made to match them, and I went to a beauty parlour and had facial massage and other things. But now all that has vanished, I no longer care about what I look like.

It is strange how often in one lifetime one changes and changes again, even an ordinary person like myself. When I look back, I see myself first as the young girl in my father's house, impatient, waiting for things to happen; then as the calm wife and mother, fulfilling all my many duties; and then again, when children are bigger and my dear husband, many years older than myself, has moved far away from me and I am more his daughter than his wife – then again I am different. In those years we mostly lived in the hills, and I would go for long walks by myself, for hours and hours, sometimes with great happiness to be there among those great green mountains in sun and mist. But sometimes also I was full of misery and longed for something as great and beautiful as those mountains to fill my own life which seemed, in those years, very empty. But when my dear husband left us for ever, I came down from the mountains and then began that fashionable town-life of which I have already spoken. But that too has finished. Now I get up in the mornings, I drink my tea, I walk round the garden with a peaceful heart; I pick a handful of blossoms· and these I lay at the feet of Vishnu in my prayer-room. Without taking my bath or changing out of the old cotton sari in which I have spent the night, I sit for many hours on the veranda, doing nothing, only looking out at the flowers and the birds. My thoughts come and go.

At about twelve o'clock Boekelman is ready and comes out of his room. He always likes to sleep late, and after that it always takes him at least one or two hours to get ready. His face is pink and shaved, his clothes are freshly pressed, he smells of shaving lotion and eau-de-Cologne and all the other things he applies out of the rows of bottles on his bathroom shelf. In one hand he has his rolled English umbrella, with the other he holds Susi on a red leather lead. He is ready to go out. He looks at me, and I can see he is annoyed at the way I am sitting there, rumpled and unbathed. If he is not in a hurry to go, he may stop and talk with me for a while, usually to complain about something; he is never in a very good mood at this time of day. Sometimes he will say the washerman did not press his shirts well, another time that his coffee this morning was stone cold; or he could not sleep all night because of noise coming from the servant quarters; or that a telephone message was not delivered to him promptly enough, or that it looked as if someone had tampered with his mail. I answer him shortly, or sometimes not at all, only go on looking out into the garden; and this always makes him angry, his face becomes very red and his voice begins to shake a little though he tries to control it:

'Surely it is not too much to ask,' he says, 'to have such messages delivered to me clearly and at the right time?' As he speaks, he stabs tiny holes into the ground with his umbrella to emphasize what he is saying. I watch him doing this, and then I say, 'Don't ruin my garden.' He stares at me in surprise for a moment, after which he deliberately makes another hole with his umbrella and goes on talking: 'It so happened it was an extremely urgent message —' I don't let him get far. I'm out of my chair and I shout at him, 'You are ruining my garden', and then I go on shouting about other things, and I advance towards him and he begins to retreat backwards. 'This is ridiculous,' he says, and some other things as well, but he can't be heard because I am shouting so loud and the dog too has begun to bark. He walks faster now in order to get out of the gate more quickly, pulling the dog along with him; I follow them, I'm very excited by this time and no longer know what I'm saying. The gardener, who is cutting the hedge, pretends not to hear or see anything but concentrates on his work. At last he is out in the street with the dog, and they walk down it very fast, with the dog turning round to bark and he pulling it along, while I stand at the gate and pursue them with my angry shouts till they have disappeared from sight.

That is the end of my peace and contemplation. Now I am very upset, I walk up and down the garden and through the house, talking to myself and sometimes striking my two fists together. I think bad things about him and talk to him in my thoughts, and likewise in my thoughts he is answering me and these answers make me even more angry. If some servant comes and speaks to me at this time, I get angry with him too and shout so loud that he runs away, and the whole house is very quiet and everyone keeps out of my way. But slowly my feelings begin to change. My anger burns itself out, and I am left with the ashes of remorse. I remember all my promises to myself, all my resolutions never to give way to my bad temper again; I remember my beautiful morning hours, when I felt so full of peace, so close to the birds and trees and sunlight and other innocent things. And with that memory tears spring into my eyes, and I lie down sorrowfully on my bed. Lakshmi, my old woman servant who has been with me nearly forty years, comes in with a cup of tea for me. I sit up and drink it, the tears still on my face and more tears rolling down into my cup. Lakshmi begins to smooth my hair, which has come undone in the excitement, and while she is doing this I talk to her in broken words about my own folly and bad character. She clicks her tongue, contradicts me, praises me, and that makes me suddenly angry again, so that I snatch the comb out of her hand, I throw it against the wall and drive her out of the room.

So the day passes, now in sorrow now in anger, and all the time I am waiting only for him to come home again. As the hour draws near, I begin to get ready. I have my bath, comb my hair, wear a new sari. I even apply a little scent. I begin to be very busy around the house, because I don't want it to be seen how much I am waiting for him. When I hear his footsteps, I am busier than ever and pretend not to hear them. He stands inside the door and raps his umbrella against it and calls out in a loud voice: 'Is it safe to come in? Has the fury abated?' I try not to smile, but in spite of myself my mouth corners twitch.

After we have had a quarrel and have forgiven each other, we are always very gay together. These are our best times. We walk round the garden, my arm in his, he smoking a cigar and I chewing a betel leaf; he tells me some funny stories and makes me laugh so much that sometimes I have to stand still and hold my sides and gasp for air, while begging him to stop. Nobody ever sees us like this, in this mood; if they did, they would not wonder, as they all do, why we are living together. Yes, everyone asks this question, I know it very well, not only my people but his too – all his foreign friends who think he is miserable with me and that we do nothing but quarrel and that I am too stupid to be good company for him. Let them see us like this only once, then they would know; or afterwards, when he allows me to come into his rooms and stay there with him the whole night.

It is quite different in his rooms from the rest of the house. The rest of the house doesn't have very much furniture in it, only some of our old things – some carved Kashmiri screens and little carved tables with mother-of-pearl tops. There are chairs and a few sofas, but I always feel most comfortable on the large mattress on the floor which is covered with an embroidered cloth and many bolsters and cushions; here I recline for hours, very comfortably, playing patience or cutting betel nuts with my little silver shears. But in his rooms there is a lot of furniture, and a radiogram and a cabinet for his records and another for his bottles of liquor. There are carpets and many pictures – some paintings of European countryside and one old oil-painting of a pink and white lady with a fan and in old-fashioned dress. There is also a framed pencil-sketch of Boekelman himself, which was made by a friend of his, a chemist from Vienna who was said to have been a very good artist but died from heatstroke one very bad Delhi summer. Hanging on the walls or standing on the mantelpiece or on little tables all over the room are a number of photographs, and these I like to look at even better than the paintings, because they are all of him as a boy or as oh! such a handsome young man, and of his parents and the hotel they owned and all lived in, in a place called Zandvoort. There are other photographs in a big album, which he sometimes allows me to look at. In this album there are also a few pictures of his wife ('Once bitten, twice shy'), which I'm very interested in; but he never lets me look at the album for long, because he is afraid I might spoil it, and he takes it away from me and puts it back in the drawer where it belongs. He is neat and careful with all his things and gets very angry when they are disarranged by the servants during dusting; yet he also insists on very thorough dusting, and woe to the whole household if he finds some corner has been forgotten. So, although there are so many things, it is always tidy in his rooms, and it would be a pleasure to go in there if it were not for Susi.

He has always had a dog, and it has always been the same very small, very hairy kind, and it has always been called Susi. This is the second Susi I have known. The first died of very old age and this Susi too is getting quite old now. Unfortunately dogs have a nasty smell when they get old, and since Susi lives in Boekelman's rooms all the time, the rooms also have this smell although they are so thoroughly cleaned every day. When you enter the first thing you notice is this smell, and it always fills me with a moment's disgust, because I don't like dogs and certainly would never allow one inside a room. But for B. dogs are like his children. How he fondles this smelly Susi with her long hair, he bathes her with his own hands and brushes her and at night she sleeps on his bed. It is horrible. So when he lets me stay in his room in the night, Susi is always there with us, and she is the only thing that prevents me from being perfectly happy then. I think Susi also doesn't like it that I'm there. She looks at me from the end of the bed with her running eyes, and I can see that she doesn't like it. I feel like kicking her off the bed and out of the room and out of the house: but because that isn't possible I try and pretend she is not there. In any case, I don't have any time for her, because I am so busy looking at B. He is usually asleep before me, and then I sit up in bed beside him and look and look my eyes out at him. I can't describe how I feel. I have been a married woman, but I have never known such joy as I have in being there alone with him in bed and looking at him: at this old man who has taken his front teeth out so that his upper lip sags over his gums, his skin is grey and loose, he makes ugly sounds out of his mouth and nose as he sleeps. It is rapture for me to be there with him.

No one else ever sees him like this. All those friends he has, all his European lady-friends – they only see him dressed up and with his front teeth in. And although they have known him all these years, longer than I have, they don't really know anything about him. Only the outer part is theirs, the shell, but what is within, the essence, that is known only to me. But they wouldn't understand that, for what do they know of outer part and inner, of the shell and of the essence! It is all one to them. For them it is only life in this world and a good time and food and drink, even though they are old women like me and should not have their thoughts on these things.

I have tried hard to like these friends of his, but it is not possible for me. They are very different from anyone else I know. They have all of them been in India for many, many years – twenty-five, thirty – but I know they would much rather be somewhere else. They only stay here because they feel too old to go anywhere else and start a new life. They came here for different reasons – some because they were married to Indians, some to do business, others as refugees and because they couldn't get a visa for anywhere else. None of them has ever tried to learn any Hindi or to get to know anything about our India. They have some Indian 'friends', but these are all very rich and important people – like maharanis and cabinet ministers, they don't trouble with ordinary people at all. But really they are only friends with one another, and they always like each other's company best. That doesn't mean they don't quarrel together, they do it all the time, and sometimes some of them are not on speaking-terms for months or even years; and whenever two of them are together, they are sure to be saying something bad about a third. Perhaps they are really more like family than friends, the way they both love and hate each other and are closely tied together whether they like it or not; and none of them has any other family, so they are really dependent on each other. That's why they are always celebrating one another's birthday the way a family does, and they are always together on their big days like Christmas or New Year. If one of them is sick, the others are there at once with grapes and flowers, and sit all day and half the night round the sick-bed, even if they have not been on speaking terms.

I know that Boekelman has been very close with some of the women, and there are a few of them who are still fond of him and would like to start all over again with him. But he has had enough of them – at least in that way, although of course he is still on very friendly terms with them and meets them every day almost. When he and I are alone together, he speaks of them very disrespectfully and makes fun of them and tells me things about them that no woman would like anyone to know. He makes me laugh, and I feel proud, triumphant, that he should be saying all this to me. But he never likes me to say anything about them, he gets very angry if I do and starts shouting that I have no right to talk, I don't know them and don't know all they have suffered; so I keep quiet, although often I feel very annoyed with them and would like to speak my mind.

The times I feel most annoyed is when there is a party in Boekelman's rooms and I'm invited there with them. They all have a good time, they eat and drink, tell jokes, sometimes they quarrel; they laugh a lot and kiss each other more than is necessary. No one takes much notice of me, but I don't mind that, I'm used to it with them; anyway, I'm busy most of the time running in and out of the kitchen to see to the preparations. I am glad I have something to do because otherwise I would be very bored only sitting there. What they say doesn't interest me, and their jokes don't make me laugh. Most of the time I don't understand what they are talking about, even when they are speaking in English – which is not always, for sometimes they speak in other languages such as French or German. But I always know, in whatever language they are speaking, when they start saying things about India. Sooner or later they always come to this subject, and then their faces change, they look mean and bitter like people who feel they have been cheated by some shopkeeper and it is too late to return the goods. Now it becomes very difficult for me to keep calm. How I hate to hear them talking in this way, saying that India is dirty and everyone is dishonest; but because they are my guests, they are in my house, I have to keep hold of myself and sit there with my arms folded. I must keep my eyes lowered, so that no one should see how they are blazing with fire. Once they have started on this subject, it always takes them a long time to stop, and the more they talk the more bitter they become, the expression on their faces becomes more and more unpleasant. I suffer, and yet I begin to see that they too are suffering, all the terrible things they are saying are not only against India but against themselves too – because they are here and have nowhere else to go – and against the fate which has brought them here and left them here, so far from where they belong and everything they hold dear.

Boekelman often talks about India in this way, but I have got used to it with him. I know very well that whenever something is not quite right – for instance, when a button is missing from his shirt, or it is a very hot day in summer – at once he will start saying how bad everything is in India. Well, with him I just laugh and take no notice. But once my eldest son, Shammi, overheard him and was so angry with him, as angry as I get with B.'s friends when I hear them talking in this way. It happened some years ago – it is painful for me to recall this occasion . . .

Shammi was staying with me for a few days. He was alone that time, though often he used to come with his whole family, his wife Monica and my three darling grandchildren. Shammi is in the army – he was still a major then, though now he is a lieutenant-colonel – which is a career he has wanted since he was a small boy and which he loves passionately. At the cadet school he was chosen as the best cadet of the year, for there was no one whose buttons shone so bright or who saluted so smartly as my Shammi. He is a very serious boy. He loves talking to me about his regiment and about tank warfare and 11·1 bore rifles and other such things, and I love listening to him. I don't really understand what he is saying, but I love his eager voice and the way he looks when he talks – just as he looked when he was a small boy and told me about his cricket. Anyway, this is what we were doing that morning, Shammi and I, sitting on the veranda, he talking and I looking sometimes at him and sometimes out into the garden, where everything was green and cool and birds bathed themselves in a pool of water that had oozed out of the hose-pipe and sunk into the lawn.

This peace was broken by Boekelman. It started off with his shouting at the servant, very loudly and rudely, as he always does; nobody minds this, I don't mind it, the servant doesn't mind it, we are so used to it and we know it never lasts very long; in any case, the servant doesn't understand what is said for it is always in English, or even some other language which none of us understands, and afterwards, if he has shouted very loudly, Boekelman always gives the servant a little tip or one of his old shirts or pair of old shoes. But Shammi was very surprised for he had never heard him shout and abuse in this way (B. was always very careful how he behaved when any of the children were there). Shammi tried to continue talking to me about his regiment, but B. was shouting so loud that it was difficult to pretend not to hear him.

But it might still have been all right and nothing would have been said and Shammi and I could have pretended to each other that nothing had been heard if Boekelman had not suddenly come rushing out on to the veranda. He held his shaving-brush in one hand, and half his face was covered in shaving lather and on the other half there was a spot of blood where he had cut himself; he was in his undervest and trousers, and the trousers had braces dangling behind like two tails. He had completely lost control of himself, I could see at once, and he didn't care what he said or before whom. He was so excited that he could hardly talk and he shook his shaving-brush in the direction of the servant, who had followed him and stood helplessly watching him from the doorway. 'These people!' he screamed. 'Monkeys! Animals!' I didn't know what had happened but could guess that it was something quite trivial, such as the servant removing a razor blade before it was worn out. 'Hundreds, thousands of times I tell them!' B. screamed, shaking his brush. 'The whole country is like that! Idiots! Fools! Not fit to govern themselves!'

Shammi jumped up. His fists were clenched, his eyes blazed. Quickly I put my hand on his arm; I could feel him holding himself back, his whole body shaking with the effort. Boekelman did not notice anything but went on shouting, 'Damn rotten backward country!' I kept my hand on Shammi's arm, though I could see he had himself under control now and was standing very straight and at attention, as if on parade, with his eyes fixed above Boekelman's head. 'Go in now,' I told B., trying to sound as if nothing very bad was happening; 'at least finish your shaving.' Boekelman opened his mouth to shout some more abuses, this time probably at me, but then he caught sight of Shammi's face and he remained with his mouth open. 'Go in,' I said to him again, but it was Shammi who went in and left us, turning suddenly on his heel and marching away with his strong footsteps. The fly-screen door banged hard behind him on its spring hinges. Boekelman stood and looked after him, his mouth still open and the soap caking on his cheek. I went up close to him and shook my fist under his nose. 'Fool!' I said to him, in Hindi and with such violence that he took a step backwards in fear. I didn't glance at him again but turned away and swiftly followed Shammi into the house.

Shammi was packing his bag. He wouldn't talk to me and kept his head averted from me while he took neat piles of clothes out of the drawer and packed them neatly into his bag. He has always been a very orderly boy. I sat on his bed and watched him. If he had said something, if he had been angry, it would have been easier; but he was quite silent, and I knew that under his shirt his heart was beating fast. When he was small and something had happened to him, he would never cry, but when I held him close to me and put my hand under his shirt I used to feel his heart beating wildly inside his child's body, like a bird in a frail cage. And now too I longed to do this, to lay my hand on his chest and soothe his suffering. Only now he was grown-up, a big major with a wife and children, who had no need of his foolish mother any more. And worse, much worse, now it was not something from outside that was the cause of his suffering, but I, I myself! When I thought of that, I could not restrain myself – a sob broke from me and I cried out 'Son!' and next moment, before I knew myself what I was doing, I was down on the ground, holding his feet and bathing them with my tears to beg his forgiveness.

He tried to raise me, but I am a strong, heavy woman and I clung obstinately to his feet; so he too got down on the floor and in his effort to raise me took me in his arms. Then I broke into a storm of tears and hid my face against his chest, overcome with shame and remorse and yet also with happiness that he was so near to me and holding me so tenderly. We stayed like this for some time. At last I raised my head, and I saw tears on his lashes, like silver drops of dew. And these tender drops on his long lashes like a girl's, which always seem so strange in his soldier's face – these drops were such a burning reproach to me that at this moment I decided I must do what he wanted desperately, he and all my other children, and what I knew he had been silently asking of me since the day he came. I took the end of my sari and with it wiped the tears from his eyes and as I did this I said, 'It's all right, son. I will tell him to go.' And to reassure him, because he was silent and perhaps didn't believe me, I said, 'Don't worry at all, I will tell him myself,' in a firm, promising voice.

Shammi went home the next day. We did not mention the subject any more, but when he left he knew that I would not break my promise. And indeed that very day I went to Boekelman's room and told him that he must leave. It was a very quiet scene. I spoke calmly, looking not at B. but over his head, and he answered me calmly, saying very well, he would go. He asked only that I should give him time to find alternative accommodation, and of course to this I agreed readily, and we even had a quiet little discussion about what type of place he should look for. We spoke like two acquaintances, and everything seemed very nice till I noticed that, although his voice was quite firm and he was talking so reasonably, his hands were slightly trembling. Then my feelings changed, and I had quickly to leave the room in order not to give way to them.

From now on he got up earlier than usual in the mornings and went out to look for a place to rent. He would raise his hat to me as he passed me sitting on the veranda, and sometimes we would have a little talk together, mainly about the weather, before he passed on, raising his hat again and with Susi on the lead walking behind him, her tail in the air. The first few days he seemed very cheerful, but after about a week I could see he was tired of going out so early and never finding anything, and Susi too seemed tired and her tail was no longer so high. I hardened my heart against them. I could guess what was happening – how he went from place to place and found everywhere that rents were very high and the accommodation very small compared with the large rooms he had had in my house all these years for almost nothing. Let him learn, I thought to myself and said nothing except 'Good morning' and 'The weather is changing fast, soon it will be winter' as I watched him going with slower and slower footsteps day after day out of the gate.

At last one day he confessed to me that, in spite of all his efforts, he had not yet succeeded in finding anything suitable. He had some hard things to say about rapacious landlords. I listened patiently but did not offer to extend his stay. My silence prompted him to stand on his pride and say that I need not worry, that very shortly he would definitely be vacating the rooms. And indeed only two days later he informed me that although he had not yet found any suitable place, he did not want to inconvenience me any further and had therefore made an alternative arrangement, which would enable him to leave in a day or two. Of course I should have answered only 'Very well' and inclined my head in a stately manner, but like a fool instead I asked, 'What alternative arrangement?' This gave him the opportunity to be stately with me; he looked at me in silence for a moment and then gave a little bow and, raising his hat, proceeded towards the gate with Susi. I bit my lip in anger. I would have liked to run after him and shout as in the old days, but instead I had to sit there by myself and brood. All day I brooded what alternative arrangement he could have made. Perhaps he was going to a hotel, but I didn't think so, because hotels nowadays are very costly, and although he is not poor, the older he gets the less he likes to spend.

In the evening his friend Lina came to see him. There was a lot of noise from his rooms and also some thumping, as of suitcases being taken down; Lina shouted and laughed at the top of her voice, as she always does. I crept half-way down the stairs and tried to hear what they were saying. I was very agitated. As soon as she had gone, I walked into his room – without knocking, which was against his strict orders – and at once demanded, standing facing him with my hands at my waist, 'You are not moving in with *Lina*?' Some of his pictures had already been removed from the walls and his rugs rolled up; his suitcases stood open and ready.

Although I was very heated, he remained calm. 'Why not Lina?' he asked, and looked at me in a mocking way.

I made a sound of contempt. Words failed me. To think of him living with Lina, in her two furnished rooms that were already overcrowded with her own things and always untidy! And Lina herself, also always untidy, her hair blonde when she remembered to dye it, her swollen ankles, and her loud voice and laugh! She had first come to India in the nineteen-thirties to marry an Indian, a boy from a very good family, but he left her quite soon – of course, how could a boy like that put up with her ways? She is very free with men, even now though she is so old and ugly, and I know she has liked B. for a long time. I was quite determined on one thing; never would I allow him to move to her place, even if it meant keeping him here in the house with me for some time longer.

But when I told him that where was the hurry, he could wait till he found a good place of his own, then he said thank you, he had made his arrangements, and as I could see with my own eyes he had already begun to pack up his things; and after he had said that, he turned away and began to open and shut various drawers and take out clothes, just to show me how busy he was with packing. He had his back to me, and I stood looking at it and longed to thump it.

The next day too Lina came to the house and again I heard her talking and laughing very loudly, and there was some banging about as if they were moving the suitcases. She left very late at night, but even after she had gone I could not sleep and tossed this side and that on my bed. I no longer thought of Shammi but only of B. Hours passed, one o'clock, two o'clock, three, still I could not sleep. I walked up and down my bedroom, then I opened the door and walked up and down the landing. After a while it seemed to me I could hear sounds from downstairs, so I crept half-way down the stairs to listen. There was some movement in his room, and then he coughed also, a very weak cough, and he cleared his throat as if it were hurting him. I put my ear to the door of his room; I held my breath, but I could not hear anything further. Very slowly I opened the door. He was sitting in a chair with his head down and his arms hanging loose between his legs, like a sick person. The room was in disorder, with the rugs rolled up and the suitcases half packed, and there were glasses and an empty bottle, as if he and Lina had been having a party. There was also the stale smoke of her cigarettes; she never stops smoking and then throws the stubs, red with lipstick, anywhere she likes.

He looked up for a moment at the sound of the door opening, but when he saw it was I he looked down again without saying anything. I tiptoed over to his armchair and sat at his feet on the floor. My hand slowly and soothingly stroked his leg, and he allowed me to do this and did not stir. He stared in front of him with dull eyes; he had his teeth out and looked an old, old man. There was no need for us to say anything, to ask questions and give answers. I knew what he was thinking as he stared in front of him in this way, and I too thought of the same thing. I thought of him gone away from here and living with Lina, or alone with his dog in some rented room; no contact with India or

Indians, no words to communicate with except 'achchha' (all right) and 'pani' (water); no one to care for him as he grew older and older, and perhaps sick, and his only companions people just like himself – as old, as lonely, as disappointed, and as far from home.

He sighed, and I said, 'Is your indigestion troubling you?' although I knew it was something worse than only indigestion. But he said yes, and added, 'It was the spinach you made them cook for my supper. How often do I have to tell you I can't digest spinach at night.' After a while he allowed me to help him into bed. When I had covered him and settled his pillows the way he liked them, I threw myself on the bed and begged, 'Please don't leave me.'

'I've made my arrangements,' he said in a firm voice. Susi, at the end of the bed, looked at me with her running eyes and wagged her tail as if she were asking for something.

'Stay,' I pleaded with him. 'Please stay.'

There was a pause. At last he said, as if he were doing me a big favour, 'Well, we'll see'; and added, 'Get off my bed now, you're crushing my legs – don't you know what a big heavy lump you are?'

None of my children ever comes to stay with me now. I know they are sad and disappointed with me. They want me to be what an old widowed mother should be, devoted entirely to prayer and self-sacrifice; I too know it is the only state fitting to this last stage of life which I have now reached. But that great all-devouring love that I should have for God, I have for B. Sometimes I think: perhaps this is the path for weak women like me? Perhaps B. is a substitute for God whom I should be loving, the way the little brass image of Vishnu in my prayer-room is a substitute for that great god himself? These are stupid thoughts that sometimes come to me when I am lying next to B. on his bed and looking at him and feeling so full of peace and joy that I wonder how I came to be so, when I am living against all right rules and the wishes of my children. How do I deserve the great happiness that I find in that old man? It is a riddle.